Cream
in My Coffee

NANCY ZIMMERMAN

HEDGEHOG HILL PRESS
An imprint of NJZ Enterprises

NJZ Enterprises
P.O. Box 3148
Anderson, Indiana 46018

www.nzbestself.com

A Hedgehog Hill Press original, 2017

Cover by Rebekah Raffield

ISBN 13: 978-0692916742

DEDICATION

This is dedicated to those who have loved in spite of the odds. In the end, love is all there ever is.

ACKNOWLEDGMENTS

Thanks to Rebekah Raffield for the wonderful cover art and Heather Harrold for editing and improving my words.

I would like to thank all of those friends of mine who have read my work and encouraged me to keep writing.

I would also like to thank all of the many wonderful romance authors whose works I have read for years. I can only hope that this addition to the genre is as well accepted.

I would also like to personally thank Bill Watson, Warren Williams, Gina Kirkland, and Brenda White for all of the many conversations we have had as I was writing this story.

Last, but certainly not least, I would like to thank Art Shead for his input and the title suggestion. His suggestions were duly noted, and I think the book is better for it.

Meeting Marie

The two officers looked like they were on a mission, and they were. First Lieutenant Charles Warren Johnson and First Lieutenant Thomas J. Martin were headed to Gate 7 to wait for Charlie's friend to arrive from Cincinnati to attend the New Year's Eve Marines' Ball. It was a tradition in the Marine corps and this was the first year the young men had been able to attend. Charlie had invited Marie to help him celebrate his recent promotion.

They looked up at the flight arrival times and confirmed that they were there in plenty of time to find Marie when she deplaned.

"Tom, I tell ya. This is one of the prettiest, nicest gals you will ever meet. She's a doll."

"So how long have you been in love?"

"With Marie??" Charlie let out a hearty laugh and hit Tom's arm with the back of his hand. "Man, I have loved her for years. She is my neighbor and actually my best friend," he continued as they got to the gate as people were exiting.

"Marie, over here!" Charlie Johnson was waving his arms to get the attention of one Lynn Marie Sinclair. Charlie was looking forward to her visit. They had been neighbors in Lexington, Kentucky for as long as he could recall. They had grown up together and were like brother and sister. He was two years older and had always been around to protect her. She, on the other hand, had always been there to keep him grounded. They had loved each other for years, but when they had discussed taking it to the romantic side of things and tried to kiss each other, Marie erupted in giggles and it kind of killed the moment. Charlie had to agree that a love affair between the two of them would never take place but the lack of one made them both treasure their friendship even more.

"Charlie!" Marie ran into his outstretched arms and wrapped her arms around him. "It is so good to see you," she added as she hugged him even closer. As she disentangled herself, she noticed the good looking young Negro observing them. She straightened her skirt and sweater after the hug and gave Tom a shy smile.

"Marie," Charlie said, "I would like for you to meet my good buddy, Thomas, J. Martin. He is going to the ball too, so you will have to be sure and save him a dance."

While Marie's parents had been raised in a very segregated society, Marie had seen many combinations of nationalities and races when she attended the University of Kentucky. She had no problem imagining being held by the good looking Thomas Martin. She blushed at the idea. "Thomas," she said as she extended her hand to shake his.

"Ma'am," he replied as their hands met. Her eyes widened, and he looked at her as they both recognized some kind of cosmic influence as their hands connected. He smiled a slow smile as he said, "I will make you a deal: If you call me Tom, I will call you Marie."

Marie blushed again as she let him know that she could do that. Charlie, however, observed the greeting with great interest. He had not seen Marie blush since the time several years ago when he had walked in on her sunbathing in her backyard with no top on. This might be a very interesting visit indeed.

"What say we get your bags and get to the hotel," Charlie broke in.

Tom could not take his eyes off Marie. Charlie hadn't exaggerated when he said she was one of the prettiest girls there was. Yes, she was certainly that. Her face was angelic, with beautiful blue eyes framed by rich chestnut hair that was cut on the short side and gave her an impish look. She was beautifully curvy. Tom could almost feel the weight of her breasts in his hands. His body responded to what he knew would be an overflowing handful. He instinctively licked his bottom lip as he imagined the feel of his lips on her nipples and as his eyes grazed her chest, he noticed the hard pebbles through her sweater. He felt himself beginning to respond and the corners of his mouth almost smiled when he saw her draw her jacket over her breasts as though she knew what he was thinking. She was bundled up for the weather so he could not tell about the rest of her shape, but he imagined that her ass would not disappoint either.

Charlie elbowed Tom, "Come on, let's get headed out. It was snowing when we came in," he said, turning to Marie. "We certainly don't want to get stranded here at Dulles."

"Charlie, hand me the car keys. I will go ahead and get the car and drive it around. There is no reason for us all to go tromping through this mess," Tom offered as they got to the door and saw the snowplows struggling with the airport drop off traffic. Combine that with the trucks attempting to keep the frontage shoveled off as the snow continued to fall, and Charlie shook his head, reached into his pocket, and pulled the keys out. "Thanks, but I had better get this, since it is a rental. If any kind of an accident would happen in this weather, they might try to stiff me and not pay damages if I am not driving. You stay with Marie, and I will be right back."

As Charlie headed out the door, Tom and Marie turned to each other, and he asked, "So, what happened back there when we shook hands?"

"You felt it too, then?"

Tom was looking into her eyes, "Oh, yes, I sensed something. I just don't know what."

"I know what you mean. It seemed like a strong sense of connection, like we had already met. I have never felt anything so strange when I have met someone before."

Tom laughed, "So, Marie, are you saying that meeting me is a strange experience for you?"

She laughed in return. "That wasn't what I meant, but I guess time will tell."

The pair exchanged some information about themselves, where they had gone to high school and college, general information that people share with each other upon meeting. As Charlie pulled the car up for them to get into, Tom put his hand on the small of Marie's back and once again, he felt her shudder as something like an electrical current ran up his arm.

Becoming Friends

Charlie maneuvered the car in the Washington, DC traffic until he arrived at the Willard Hotel. Tom and Charlie had agreed that they would take advantage of their service perks and book a suite at the Willard for Marie's stay. Even though Quantico was nearby, the men had enough rank that they were entitled to stay off base with permission. Both men knew that they were due to be sent to Saigon in two weeks and it would be a long time before they had the chance to enjoy the luxury the Willard had to offer.

"Oh, my gosh!" Marie gasped. "You can't mean that we will be staying here?"

"That is exactly what we mean," Charlie said. "I haven't told you yet, but I am going to be sent to another tour in Vietnam. Tom is too. We will be leaving in a couple of weeks, so this is for us as much as it is for you."

"Do your parents know yet?" Marie said with concern in her voice.

"Yes, they are coming down next week and will stay to see me off. They knew that Tom and I had been looking forward to this ball... and, they knew you had too. Mom said that she and Linda had been on several trips to Cincinnati to meet you and shop for the perfect dress."

Marie smiled, "Yes, and it is a beauty."

"Honey," he said, "You would look great in a gunny sack."

"Hmmpf! NOW you tell me. Just think of all the shopping time I could have stayed."

They all laughed as the valets scrambled to open doors and help them with the luggage. Tom reached in and tipped them as they went through the doors into the magnificent foyer. Marie knew her mouth was gaping and she looked like a rube as she tried to take it all in. Tom and Charlie had already seen much of the world, but they looked at each other in a way that indicated this was by far the most magnificent hotel they had been in. "It is magnificent," Marie murmured as she continued to look around. "Are you sure you guys want to stay here?" she was wondering if she had brought enough money to pay for her share.

"Marie, this is our treat to you for agreeing to fly here and escort both of us to the ball."

Marie looked from Charlie to Tom then back to Charlie. She choked as she asked, "I am going to be going with both of you? How does that work?"

"Well," Tom drawled. "You just put your left hand in the crook of Charlie's right arm and your right hand in the crook of my left arm, and we all three walk in at the same time."

Marie looked at Tom with a twinkle in her eye. "Oh, well, I can do that with no problems whatsoever. I just thought it might mean I would have to dance with both of you at the same time."

"No, Sweetie, we can take turns on that account," Charlie said as he wiggled his eyebrows at her in a suggestive way.

Marie slapped him on the arm as she told him he needed to calm down and they all continued in to get checked in.

The suite had an understated elegance and contained two bedrooms which each contained two large beds. The guys told Marie to take the room that had the larger bathroom and they would share the smaller room and bath. The men knew that ladies liked private facilities, and they had spent their lives for the last several years sharing any space available with many other men. Even the smaller room would seem like total privacy to both of them.

Once they all had bags unpacked for the next week they gathered in the living room of the suite. Because the men were in the service, there were some perks included that most people were not privy to. The contents of the small bar, both the snacks and the drinks, were included in the price of the suite. They also had free room service meals if they wished to use them.

Marie had changed into a pair of jeans and a loose sweatshirt, as had the guys. Tom and Charlie were enjoying a beer as Marie entered from her room. Tom's cock jerked as he caught a glimpse of her ass in those jeans. "Oh, my God," he thought. "I have never wanted to grab an ass any more than I have now." His dick jumped again and began hardening. He adjusted himself in his seat and began thinking of what a cold shower on his growing erection would do and he got himself under control, until he looked over and saw her bent over and looking into the small refrigerator to see what soft drinks were available.

"Oh, geez," he moaned as he squirmed in his seat.

Charlie looked over with a grin, "What was that?"

"Shut up!" Tom retorted, knowing that Charlie was getting a kick out of observing his reaction to Marie. "I don't need your shit, Charlie."

"Payback is hell, isn't it?"

Charlie was referring to a similar episode where he had seen a woman that had caused his body to react similarly. Charlie had made the mistake of going over to ask her for a date not realizing that her husband had come up behind them and was listening to the query. Evidently, they were both used to her being asked out by random horny young men so he had only suffered a rejection and not a black eye.

"This is different," Tom told him very quietly. "You were right, she is special."

Charlie could not be happier at the thought of the two people who meant the most to him getting together, but he gave an involuntary shudder at the leaps they would have to take if they were going to make it more than a brief interaction.

Right now, the threesome was hungry and they perused the room service menu to look for their dinner choices.

It was still snowing when the room service waiter brought up their order, and the floor-to-ceiling windows gave them a gorgeous view as they sat and enjoyed the steaks that had been grilled to perfection along with the salads and baked potatoes that accompanied them. They discussed what sights they might take advantage of if it continued to snow, such as the construction taking place turning the Natural Cultural Center into the Kennedy Center for the Performing Arts. It was a $23 million renovation as a tribute to the late President John Kennedy.

They decided to see a movie, and, after much discussion, they narrowed it down to *The Graduate* and then called a cab rather than risk the roads themselves.

When the movie ended, many points of it provoked discussion, but they had more discussion about a preview they saw for the newly released *Guess Who's Coming to*

Dinner with Sidney Poitier, Katharine Hepburn and Spencer Tracy. It was considered one of the most significant movies of the year since it followed on the heels of the Loving v. Virginia decision in June of that year. Until the Supreme Court made their decision, it was illegal in many states for people of two different races to marry. As Marie watched the trailer, she felt the tears well in her eyes. With very little effort, her attraction to Tom was so great she saw that she could easily fall in love with him. They had only touched and yet the desire to get to know him better was so strong she knew she was vulnerable.

Tom knew first-hand how the race game was played. He had a cousin who had married a white girl. It had been an uphill battle for them both. Neither set of parents had been in favor of it. Strangely enough, it was not because there was an issue by itself, but rather because of society's perception of it. You had to be very brave to enter into that kind of relationship. As he looked over at Marie, he realized that if there was ever a white girl who could make him color blind, it would be Marie Sinclair.

The discussion led them to decide they would see that movie the next evening, but for tonight they were content to get another drink ready and play some cards before they retired.

Later, Marie lay in her bed and reached up to her nipples. They hardened as she thought about how her body had reacted to Tom. She had become wet as her hand brushed over his smooth arm. The beauty of their different colored skin caused her to tremble and consider how his beautiful dark body would look naked next to hers in bed, and she imagined his hands roaming over her body. She had never thought about color in a way that would entice physical response. She had never had close Negro friends, although she had sat next to them in choir when she was in high school. She thought about the preview they had seen this evening and how her parents would react if she brought Tom home for dinner. She tossed and turned for a while before she decided to get up and get some ice water.

She had a night shirt on and didn't bother putting on a robe just to get a drink. She gave a small gasp when she went around the corner and ran into a hard object. Tom reached out and grabbed her before she fell on the floor.

"Are you okay, Marie?"

"Oh, yes," she stammered. "I'm sorry, I didn't realize anyone was even up. I just came out to get a drink of water."

"You were having trouble sleeping too?" he asked very quietly.

"Ah... yeah, I was."

"Me too. You know why I was having trouble sleeping?"

Marie looked up into Tom's eyes. There was enough light from the dimmed canned fixtures in the entry of the suite for her to see the intensity with which he was looking at her.

He stepped closer to her and put a hand on her waist. She didn't stop him but rather stepped closer and put her hand on his arm. He pulled her closer, and her hand traveled up his arm and around his neck as his other hand circled her waist. They embraced as their lips met. Marie felt a gush of moisture from her core like she had never experienced as they kissed.

Tom pulled her even closer and his hands roamed down to cup her beautiful ass.

He pulled her into his hardening cock so she could see just what she did to him and understand why he couldn't sleep.

She pulled her lips away from his. "Oh, Tom. We shouldn't be doing this."

"And why not? We both want this, don't we. Tell me you don't want this as much as I do, and I will walk away."

"No," she said as she gripped his arm. "I do want this. I don't understand what my body is feeling. I have never felt this way."

"Never?" he asked.

"Never," she replied. "My body is responding to you when I look at you, when I even think about kissing you or touching you. It scares me."

"Does is scare you because I am a black man?" he asked. He was afraid of the answer, but if they stood a chance, he had to know.

She put her head on his chest and just let him hold her. "No, don't be silly. I only think about your skin when I look at it and think about what a beautiful tone it is. Why?"

"Then I am not sure what it is that is scaring you."

"You make me want to do things. Things I have read about. Things I had decided I would not do until I was married." She hoped he would not ask her any more. She was a virgin and until she had met Tom she had no clue that her body could respond like that. It never had, so how would she know?

"Just so you know, Marie, you make me want to do things, too. Can I kiss you again?"

She lifted her head off his chest, turned her lips upward, and pulled herself toward him. They kissed, this time with a fire that caused them to moan trying to get closer. Tom reached down, hefted her up into his arms, and carried her to the couch where he sat down with her on his lap.

She maneuvered herself so that she was straddling him. He had not put a shirt on, so he felt her hard nipples rub against his bare chest. She did, too, and she pushed into him more as she moaned. He cupped her ass and pulled her into his erection as felt her moistness through her skimpy panties. She felt like she was not even in her body. It began responding by rocking her pussy into the erection in a way that soothed her yet

17

caused her to move more quickly. She felt her body building up for some kind of a release. She felt herself releasing moisture. Tom moaned as she moved. His hips began moving rhythmically with hers. She could not tell who was moaning; she only knew that as their tongues began to explore each other's mouths and their bodies moved against each other, she was nearing some kind of explosion that she did not understand. When Tom reached up under her t-shirt, took her nipples in his big hands, and pinched them, she bucked her hips and exploded, feeling empty as her muscles contracted. "There should be something there," she thought, "and that something should have been Tom." She now understood where she was and who she was.

He released her ass, wrapped his arms around her, and just sat holding her. He waited until she was asleep then took her into her room, placed her on the bed, and covered her up, tenderly kissing her temple. "Good night, Baby," he whispered.

As he headed to the bathroom to take a quick cold shower, Charlie said, "You treat her right, buddy, or you have me to deal with. You can count on that."

Charlie rolled over, and Tom went on into the bathroom to take himself in hand and imagine it was Marie surrounding him--first her hand, then her mouth, and then her beautifully wet pussy--until he came all over the side of the shower stall.

Guess Who's Coming to Dinner

Everyone got up late the next morning and ordered room service. Since there had been about a foot of snow over the previous two days, they spent the morning watching television and playing cards.

Later that afternoon they got dressed to go out to dinner and see the movie they had previously decided to see. Tom and Marie had not had an opportunity to talk about what had happened the previous evening, but they both seemed comfortable around each other, so it was a conversation they could have the next time they were alone together.

While the movie was presented as a drama, there were some funny moments in it that provided some comic relief and kept a serious topic from being preachy in its approach.

Charlie and Marie admitted that their parents would probably act like the Draytons, the prejudiced family in the movie, not because they had a particular prejudice against blacks but because interracial marriages were not common and they had not had interracial friendships themselves. It would be out of their comfort zone. Tom felt like his parents would be more open simply because there were already whites in his family structure. They had already had to face those issues in his family.

Marie found herself picturing her mother and father's responses, and it did not set well with her. She determined she was going to have to begin having some dialogue with them about this issue.

The next two days flew by. Tom and Marie had no more opportunity to be alone, and Marie made sure to take water with her to bed so that she would not risk running into Tom in the middle of the night. She ached for him but she felt like avoiding the temptation right now might be the best course of action.

The morning before the ball Charlie was called back to Quantico for a briefing. He had been assured he would be back by mid-afternoon. He left a message for Tom and Marie that he would not be back before 2 pm, maybe later. Being called back to base worked out well, as he felt that he needed to get out of the way so that Tom and Marie could discuss their feelings about each other.

Tom arose, showered, and found Charlie's note propped against the phone. He had not heard the phone and was surprised that he had not been called in also. He couldn't help but wonder if Charlie was letting them have some time to themselves. If that was the case, he was going to owe Charlie big time. Even the idea of being alone with Marie caused his dick to twitch. He reached down and gave himself a couple of pumps, just because the idea of her hands around him had caused him to begin hardening. He decided he needed to slip back into the shower quickly and take care of himself so that he would not get an embarrassing hard-on when Marie came out of the bedroom.

Tom turned the slow water on and began long slow strokes. He wanted to enjoy the feeling. He was usually a pump and cum guy to get the release out so he could go on, but this time he wanted to enjoy the fantasy. He was enjoying the continual build before streams of cum hit the wall and he watched his seeds wash down the drain. He was conflicted as hell over this woman. How could he be so smitten so soon?

He toweled off and put clothes on. Marie was reading the paper when he returned to the living room. While he had been showering, she had called down for coffee, danish, a couple of omelettes, some sausage, bacon, and biscuits and gravy. Those delights were spread on the table along with some selections of juices and other additions as was the custom of the Willard.

The two sat in companionable silence enjoying their breakfast and their newspapers. Tom walked over and turned on the television. "One day, it is my goal to have a television in my kitchen so I can enjoy watching the news and eating my breakfast every morning," he said.

"Seriously, that is your dream?"

"Well, one of them. It involves being married to a sexy-as-hell woman, enjoying morning sex before we get out of bed, having her wash my back then letting me wash hers, changing diapers on our children while she gets the bottle ready. You know, things like that."

Marie was stunned. To have a man that would actually change a diaper would be amazing. Those friends of hers who had children had husbands who would literally leave the house in order to avoid changing diapers.

"You would change diapers?"

"Why wouldn't I?"

"I didn't think men did that."

"A real man will change diapers and help his wife, Doll, and don't you ever settle for one who won't."

Marie smiled and he smiled back. "I will remember that," she said.

Tom got up to get more coffee and brought back the pot to refill hers. "More for you?"

She nodded, "Yes, thanks."

"You need anything else while I am up?" he asked.

"You might bring me a couple of pieces of bacon," she said.

He picked up three pieces and took a bite of one. He handed her the other two, and she took them, thanking him. She then bit into one of the pieces herself.

He looked thoughtful. "What?" she said.

"Do you realize how many people in this world would not even eat something that a black man had touched?"

"No, I don't. And I am not one of them."
With that comment, she turned back to the
paper.

About 10 that morning, Charlie called to
tell Tom and Marie that he would be tied up
until about 5 that afternoon, getting back in
time to get dressed and get to the ball at 8
that evening.

"What are we going to do today?" Marie
asked Tom.

"I have an idea," he said with a glint in
his eyes. "Come here."

"I am not sure I should."

He was sitting on the couch, fully
dressed with sweats and a t-shirt. She had
jeans and a t-shirt on so she went over to him.
He reached up and pulled her down straddling
him. "We could do what we did the other
night, I rather liked that."

"You didn't get satisfied. Why would
you want to do that again?" she asked.

"Because I got to watch you get
satisfied. This time, I might show you how to
satisfy me."

Marie's body had already decided this
was a great idea because without realizing it,
she was rubbing up against his erection. She

wished she didn't have jeans on, only underwear, but she was too embarrassed to say anything.

Tom seemed to read her mind. "Let's get those jeans off of you first, and I am going to take these sweats off. We will both have underwear on. Nothing is going to happen that we don't decide on together."

Marie made a bold move as she removed both her jeans and her bra under her t-shirt. Tom removed his sweats and his shirt and sat with his briefs on. Marie looked down and saw his erection bulging just waiting for her to rub up against him. She felt herself release juices and her panties were wet. Tom's eyes widened as he noticed the wet spot. He was going to have to taste a bit of that honey before the day was over, but he didn't want to scare her. He felt his cock twitch and get even larger. Marie noticed and sat down on the hard rod. She began rubbing back and forth as she straddled him on her knees.

Once again he cupped her ass and groaned because it felt so good in his hands. He brought his hands around to the front of her legs and moved them slowly to her inner thighs. He moved his thumbs up under the panty line toward her clit. Marie was moving slowly with her eyes closed. When Tom's thumb touched her pearly nub, her eyes popped open with a smile on her face. "Oh, god, Tom. That feels so good. Don't stop, please."

Tom had no intention of stopping as his hips began moving faster. He took his thumbs away from her clit and put them back around her ass and directed her to move faster. She leaned down toward him and they began kissing, getting closer and closer to release. "I am going to shoot my wad too, baby. You just take your time, but we are both going to get off this time."

"I want to know what to do to satisfy you, Tom."

"Just keep riding me, honey." They both moved faster and their breathing became more erratic the closer they got to their climax. Tom pumped his hips into her in quicker and quicker motions. He reached up to take one of her nipples in his mouth. That was all it took for both of them to erupt. Marie kept riding to bring herself back down, and Tom enjoyed her movements too.

When they had both slowed, he moved her off of him and stood up. He reached for her hand and they showered together, and as their excitement grew again, he led her to the bedroom. He laid out a condom, just in case, but he told her he had something else in mind.

He instructed her to lay down on her back. His head went directly to her pussy began exploring. She responded to his attention so well that he hardened again. The more he licked her pussy, the more she moaned and the more she moved. She fisted the sheets as she began moving in rhythm while he thrust his tongue inside her folds. She moaned his name with every thrust. She kept telling him to keep going. She knew she was coming, but it wasn't happening as fast as she wanted it to. Tom told her to enjoy the build up. He let her know he was going to make sure she came and that he just wanted her to enjoy it all.

"Oh, my god," Marie thought as she enjoyed every swipe of Tom's tongue. She was so wet it was embarrassing, but Tom seemed to love it. He would add his juices to her juices and seem to slurp them up. Then he would do something with his fingers up inside her that made her feel like she was releasing a lot of juices. He told her to keep squirting, but she didn't even know what that meant. She only knew that she wasn't sure how long she could keep feeling this good without the release of an orgasm. She had not known what one felt like until a few days ago. Now she wanted them all the time.

"AAAhhh, Tom, ... oh, God, Tom... I'm coming... oh, god."

"Baby, you taste so good. Juice some more, baby. Give me something to lick up." He put his fingers up to reach that spot that caused her to squirt. He got one more good taste before she came down from her climax.

Marie was worn out. She felt like all of her bones were gone. She had not strength to move. She simply laid there like a blob with no sense of structure or form.

"Tom, how do you know how to do all that?"

"I have had some experience that you haven't had. Let's leave it at that. But I have never enjoyed seeing anyone come more than I have you."

"But Tom, can I taste you? Can I do to you what you just did to me? Will it make you feel good?"

The idea of Marie's lips and mouth around his cock was about more than he could take. He had remained hard as he ate her and although it had gone down a bit after she was done, just the thought of her coming down on him made it rock hard again.

He laid back on the bed with his cock jutting out. "You do whatever you feel like doing and I guaran-damn-tee you I will love it," he told her.

She looked at his big dick and noticed drops on it. She leaned down and licked the drops off of the slit, and he pushed his hips up as he moaned. She gathered that he liked it, so she got a little bolder. She licked at the head of his cock and took him in her mouth. At the same time, she put her hand around his organ near the base and began stroking as she put her mouth around the top of his dick. Up and down she went as he began pumping in rhythm with her. "Marie, keep that up, keep that up... I am building up... Oh, honey... keep it up... You feel so good... oh,yeah..."

He kept moving and so did she. She loved the way he tasted, and she enjoyed watching him enjoy what she was doing. She kept up, taking him a little deeper each time. He kept pumping, and she reached to feel his balls. She played with them too as he moaned even more. She could sense his breathing get more irregular. "Oh... Marie... I am going to come..."

She knew he was trying to tell her to take her mouth off of him, but she wanted to taste all of him. So she just pumped her mouth a bit quicker and deeper until she felt the spurts of cum fill her mouth. She swallowed what she could and what she couldn't swallow, she licked off his dick after her mouth released him.

Tom and Marie slept wrapped up in each other's arms after leaving a wake up call with the desk. They did not want Charlie to walk in on them, and they needed to be getting dressed by 4 that afternoon. It was difficult for them to separate when they got the phone call, but both were so spent from the morning that they managed to keep their hands off of each other so that they were dressing by the time Charlie came back.

All it took was one look at both of them for Charlie to know they were in love and had been expressing that love all afternoon. He was happy for them even though he knew they would be fighting an uphill battle against the prejudice and bigotry that still existed in the United States.

Cinderella's Ball

When Marie came out of her room both
Tom and Charlie's jaws dropped. They stood
up gaping at her transformation. She had put
her hair up in an elaborate sophisticated style.
Her dress was a satin floor length ball gown.
While it looked strapless, there was a nude
lace yoke that was round-necked and
sleeveless. With the chiffon overlay on the
skirt, the overall look was like that of royalty.
The teal color brought out her hair and skin
tones beautifully and added to the
sophistication.

"Marie, you look stunning, absolutely
stunning," Charlie told her as walked around
her. She turned her back toward him so he
could finish zipping her up.

Tom felt his temperature flare as he
watched Charlie comfortably zip her up. He
supposed they were comfortable enough over
the years that they had probably seen each
other in different states of undress and
thought nothing of it. Somehow, that didn't set
well with him. She was his and he wanted no
other man's hands on her. Wait, where had
that come from? They were not nearly to that

exclusive stage, were they? Yes, he reasoned, they were. He only hoped he would have time to discuss that with her before they parted in a few days. Right now she was here, and he would be spending this evening with her and Charlie in one of the most talked-about social events of the year.

He just kept looking at her until she snapped her fingers close to his face. "Tom. Tom. Are you okay?"

"My dear, Marie. I am more than okay. I am rendered speechless by your beauty." He reached for her hand and brought her knuckles to his mouth and kissed them, then pulled her into his arms, kissed her cheek, then let her go. "You look beautiful," he smiled.

"You two are certainly good for a girl's ego, I will give you that," she said smiling. "So, Charlie, did your mom do a good job helping me shop?"

"I will have to give her an A+ on shopping," he chuckled.

"I am glad it meets with your approval," she looked at them both and continued, "Both of your approvals. Now, isn't it time we went downstairs and got this shindig going?"

They left the suite and headed for the elevator. They got on and when the elevator reached the fourth floor, it stopped and let another couple on then continued on to the main floor.

There were attendants at the doors of the elevator to escort the officers to the Grand Ballroom. There were several military parties all over the Washington, DC area. Some felt it was in poor taste to have these balls while the country was engaged in warfare, but the other factions stated that some kind of relief was needed for morale.   There was always some kind of controversy concerning the balls and they always seemed to survive. This year was no different.

The music playing were old standards, the kind you would hear Glenn Miller Band play. There were smaller rooms off to the side where different music played from some of the more current hits, classical string quartets, and jazz ensembles. They visited all of the rooms and stopped frequently to greet people they knew and introduce Marie as a friend to them both from Kentucky. Tom's hand would go to the small of her back on occasion when she sensed that he felt someone was looking at her a little longer or a little more closely than he wanted them to. It seemed to be a territorial move and Marie didn't mind a bit. She would place a possessive hand on his lower arm when a woman let her eyes stray a bit longer than Marie liked, too.

It was about 1 am when Tom noticed Marie's energy waning. He spoke quietly to Charlie and while Charlie stayed, Marie and Tom went upstairs. Tom took his attire off while Marie stripped down to exquisite underwear complete with a garter belt. She had no bra on due to the style of the dress. Tom stumbled and nearly fell as he was getting out of his trousers. "Holy mother of Jesus, Marie. You have been like that under that dress all evening?"

Marie chuckled as she looked and could tell that he liked what he was seeing as he seemed to grow right in front of her. She licked her lips and his cock jumped as if to say, "Here I am baby, come kiss me."

"You like?" She turned around and bent over with her hands on her knees and looked back at him over her shoulder. "Well, Tom, do you?"

He growled a low growl as he finished tearing his clothes off and stood stark naked and began slowly walking toward her. "You don't know just who you are messing with, Missy," he said in a low tone as he continued closing the gap between them.

"I am ready for anything you have for me," she said as she reached into her panties and pulled out a foil square. "I even came prepared in case we didn't make it back up here before we had to have each other."

Tom gave a loud laugh, "Marie, you are some kind of wicked. I take that back, you are my kind of wicked." He almost professed his love for her right then and there, but now wasn't the time to scare her off.

He put his hands out on her hips and pulled her ass toward his erection. He spread her cheeks and rubbed his hard cock between them as he reached around and ripped the panties off from under the garter belt leaving her totally exposed to his hands. He began kneading her mound causing her to back into him further to get closer to him. He leaned over and said, "Let's take this to the bed. Charlie knows I am going to be in here all night so we will not be disturbed."

Marie walked over and placed her hands and knees on the bed then stopped with her ass in the air so Tom could do whatever he wanted to. He played with her pussy getting her wetter and wetter. He pushed her down so she was on her elbows with her ass high as he got under her and began licking and sucking up all those pussy fluids he loved to taste. He put first one finger, then another in her to help prepare her for intercourse. She was certainly ready enough. He then rolled her over on her back and climbed next to her. He began with her breasts and made love to them, kneading them and taking the rock-hard nipples in his mouth, sucking on them alternately while kneading the other. She did indeed have a generous handful and the more he sucked, the hotter she got. His hands roamed down her stomach, seeking out her pussy while she reached up and put her hand around his cock, stroked down, then took his balls tenderly in her hand to play with them for a while. Their foreplay was not rushed this evening. It was exploratory, and it was an effort on both their parts to discover what the other liked that would bring them the most pleasure. Tom made love to Marie and Marie made love to Tom until they could neither stand it any longer. Tom tore the square foil packet open with his teeth, rolled the condom on, and slowly entered her.

He met with no resistance since she was so thoroughly prepared for him. They began slowly and the pace of their thrusts got more heated and they soon began pumping into each other with a frenzy that guaranteed a rich explosion at the climax of their lovemaking. Neither of them were quiet as they came, and the intensity was so great that as Tom rested inside her as she came down from her climax, he felt himself harden again. He removed his dick and took care of the condom then went to his pants pocket and took out the strip that he had put there earlier, donned another one and went back to Marie and entered her again, only to bring her twice more to climax before he released himself.

They slept, but Marie began stroking Tom in the middle of the night and he awoke only to turn over and make love with her again. They fell asleep in each other's arms again and slept until it was light. Marie rolled over and saw that it was already 10 am. She was going to have to be at Dulles, ready to get on the flight home, in only twenty-four hours. She was not quite sure how she was ever going to leave this man she had come to love. Yes, she realized, she did love him. It was intense, it was real, and in some circles it was unacceptable, but she loved him.

Tet Offensive

It was January 21st when they arrived in Saigon with orders that would have them working in the capitol for about a year. It was nearing the TET holiday which meant there would be a truce for the Vietnamese New Year celebration.

Tom and Charlie's commander decided to send them both to the village of Xuan Loc, about forty miles northeast of Saigon. They arrived on January 25th and began setting up the field office. While the men shared the same rank, Tom had achieved it three years earlier than Charlie and would be expected to get to Captain within the next six months. He was given the lead on this deployment and the two men worked with great synchronization to get the job done within the first week they were there.

The tide of popular opinion in the United States had drastically changed since 1965. At that time about 25% believed that the United States had made a mistake sending troops to Vietnam. As of December, when the two friends left the states, that percentage had jumped to 45%. Briefings in November had indicated that 55% of the citizens thought there should be a tougher war policy. Statistics had been parlayed on newscasts to indicate that the tide was turning against the Viet Cong, but from the intel that filtered through Tom's hand, that was not the case. It had not helped that General William Westmoreland had indicated to a TIME reporter that he hoped the North made an attack because the South was ready for a fight.

The last half of 1967 there had been much information collected by the intelligence agencies to indicate from troop movements by the North that they were planning some significant movements against the South. Hanoi announced in October, however, that it would observe the seven-day truce from January 27th to February 3rd to celebrate the TET holiday.

The South Vietnamese military therefore was going to give a recreational leave to about half its force during that time. Westmoreland tried to get him to rescind the order, but President Thieu felt that if they had been recalled it would have been bad for morale.

For the last quarter of 1967, Tom and Charlie were deeply briefed about Saigon and surrounding community military activity. The Marines had suffered some large losses and there had been a significant Marine battle at Khe Sanh on the very day the two friends had arrived on transport in Saigon.

"We sure got sent here at a helluva time," Tom said as he opened a beer and handed it to Charlie.

"Yeah, what do you think of this after all the troop movement we have been advised of over the last couple of months?"

"Personally," said Tom, "I think this battle at Khe Sanh is the tip of the iceberg and I think it is a distraction. Think about it... a major offensive less than a week before an announced truce? What are the chances? Nope, I think something is up, I just can't figure out exactly what."

"You gotta look at it objectively. From a strategic standpoint, this isn't going to be some hit and run battle. Every battle gets drawn out for months. There are these small engagements between the Cong and the South where everybody shoots off a lot of rounds, men are killed, sometimes collateral damage to small villages, but this was a distinct strike, meant to cripple the people and feed the propaganda mill. There are some other factors in play, I agree."

The night of January 30, 1968, Tom and Charlie finished their beers and headed to bed, not realizing that the world was soon going to seem be spinning much faster. They would soon be privy to viewing some of those "other factors" that Charlie mentioned.

The men were awakened about 2 am to the sound of villagers screaming and gunfire. They grabbed their M16 rifles and shouted to the villagers to go to the armory. The villagers had divided themselves in groups with heads of each group in charge of communications with the Marine military command. It was a new concept that had been put in place when Tom and Charlie arrived. They had thought about waiting until they were more well-recognized and accepted in the small city, but decided against it when the leaders came to them the second day they were there, offering to help them establish a command post. It was a good thing that the training had begun when Charlie hurried across the courtyard and saw fifteen men already gathered there to receive the guns and ammunition to fight those that were attacking them. As Charlie unlocked the door, more men came running over, and he waved to one he knew as Anh Dung to help with the distribution.

The men took arms away as others arrived. There were seven arsenals such as this with smaller posts around the town. Charlie reached for the walkie talkie to communicate with the others, but only five answered. The other two were silent, and Charlie thought of the ramifications if they had already been captured by the enemy. One of the spots was small near the north edge of town. It would seem to be the last outpost if the offensive was coming in from the southeast, as had been the supposed tactical presumption. If, however, the attack was coming from the north, it would be the first site attacked. The other arsenal was in the middle of the area and regardless of the direction of attack, would be the very last one to get overrun.

Tom showed up a few minutes later to help. He had taken the plans to the Captain and received permission to continue the dispersal of munitions to the South

Vietnamese military that showed up. Thanks to the President's dictate, many of the men were out of town visiting relatives in nearby villages. Those men were like sitting ducks, unable to return to the area where arms were readily available. They had limited munitions, and because they thought that the truce would actually be a reality, many had only the barest of essentials with them.

The bombing was intense but intermittent. They experienced a wave of assaults, then there might be nothing for two or three days. Scouts were sent into the countryside to gather information and report on troop activity. When they came back, all of the officers would set up maps indicating the direction and size of the platoons. The children were sequestered in the churches and hospitals. According to rules of worldwide engagement, hospitals, churches, and schools were agreed upon to be left alone. For some reason, however, schools had not been deemed safe since three had been hit directly in Saigon earlier in the war.

The fighting continued through February. It was evident that what had been observed in the last part of 1967 as far as repositioning the Viet Cong troops was preparation for this attack. The Viet Cong were winning the war unless a counter attack could be launched.

Injuries

February 10, 1968 and the Cong were ramping up their attacks. Several of the strongholds had been taken by the American troops, but there were some that were still fighting. Xuan Loc was still under siege, and it laid in the valley in such a way that supplies could be obtained only from Saigon or from the air.

What made it difficult in some ways worked to their advantage in other ways. If the Americans could not get supplies, then neither could the Viet Cong. Also, the allies were becoming surrounded. Two towns within a twenty mile radius had a freer route to supplies and munitions. The villagers in those towns had overrun and captured their attackers in the last week and were beginning to funnel supplies into Xuan Loc.

Navy battleships were in the area and had pretty well cleared the area east of the quadrant where Xuan Loc was. Communications had become intermittent, and while there had been visits by some of those in charge of the retaliation, for the most part, the Marines at Xuan Loc were on their own and under the command of Tom, Charlie, and the Captain in charge of the outpost. Tom and Charlie were quick learners, which had been crucial in preventing them from being quickly taken over. The classes on strategy that Tom had taught as an assistant when he was waiting on assignment after his first deployment had gone a long way to keep them from being overrun by the Cong.

News came to the Marines on April 4th that the Reverend Dr. Martin Luther King, Jr. had been assassinated. Tom had been in the Academy when the march on Washington had taken place. He had seen Reverend King deliver his famous "I Have a Dream" speech. He was fighting for a country that he held out hope for. He wanted, more than anything, for that day to arrive when white children and black children would play together, work together, and live side by side as neighbors. He wanted the time to come when it was not looked down upon when a black man loved and married a white woman. He wanted to know that when he and Marie had children, those children would be judged for their character and not by the darkness of their skin. It was a dream that many people of all ethnicities shared, and he only hoped the dream had not died with Dr. King.

Even though the fighting for the offensive during TET was over, the barrage continued throughout the spring. It was early in May that the citizens heard yet another incoming plane. Thought to be Viet Cong, people took cover. It was followed by the sound of another plane approaching. This time it was one of the American planes, so the people relaxed. It was their hope that it it would take down the North's plane then bomb the outlying areas to rid the countryside of any more who were coming to help the Viet Cong troops already there. If they could cut off the supply of troops, then the Marines could advance to take those pockets of Cong within the city limits.

Unfortunately, the North Vietnamese plane continued in, low over the city, and they let go with the worst shelling the town had seen. Two small girls, who had gotten away from their mother as she had gone to pick up food during the lull in activity, were stranded and exposed. Charlie ran across the street, scooped them up, and ran for cover. They were almost under cover when a bomb hit the building next to him. He covered the girls with his body and dove into some of the overgrowth.

There was no additional fire as the plane continued on out toward the South China Sea. The American plane fired and the Vietnamese plane went up in an explosive ball of fire. The men on the ground ran to help Charlie and pull debris off of him. They called for the medics to come and get him to the hospital. The girls were scared but safe and were handed off to their mother.

The ambulance arrived quickly, Charlie was loaded carefully, and headquarters was notified. He had been started with a saline drip and oxygen. There were massive contusions on his arms and his forehead was bleeding as the medics worked to get it stopped. They pulled into the emergency entrance and wheeled him into the building where Tom was waiting.

Dr. Lahn Nguyen came out five hours later with news for Tom. Charlie had sustained some internal damage and had his spleen removed. He had suffered two broken ribs and his lung had collapsed twice during surgery. He had a fractured humerus and a rather severe concussion. The doctor was more concerned about his optic nerve. With the equipment they had there, they could find no damage, but the reason it had taken him so long to report to Tom was that he had been waiting for Charlie to wake up. Charlie was blind. The doctor thought it was traumatic blindness that would resolve itself, but he wanted to send him back stateside to Walter Reed for further diagnosis and possible treatment. Tom signed the papers then went into the room to visit his friend.

Charlie laid there, eyes closed, his arm, head, and midriff all bandaged.

"Well, I gotta hand it to you, buddy, you certainly found an inventive way to meet some cute nurses," Tom said in an attempt to engage his friend.

Charlie continued to keep his eyes closed although Tom knew he was not asleep.

"Hey, Charlie, I just signed the papers to give you a vacation in the states. The least you can do is thank me."

"Thanks," mumbled Charlie. "Now get the hell out of here and leave me the fuck alone."

"Nope, not the way it works. You see, you have been banged up pretty well. There is something wrong with your optic nerve and you have to get back to the states to let the specialists look at it so that the blindness you are experiencing now will not become permanent, ya hear? And, for your information, I just got notice that I am now promoted to Captain, so that makes me your boss and you can't be disrespectful to your superior."

Charlie perked up at that news, "Well, you dog, congratulations Captain. Now, get the hell out of here and leave me the fuck alone."

Tom laughed. He had tried to put himself in Charlie's place, and he knew that he would be mad as hell if the same thing happened to him. They were friends for life and you just didn't ditch a friend when they were down. He knew Charlie would come around, but he wasn't sure when. "You will be on your way to Walter Reed within twenty-four hours. I will be notifying both your parents and the lovely Marie Sinclair. I am sure they will be glad to know that your grumpy ass is going to be okay. Now, I will see you before you muster out. Get some rest, buddy."

As Charlie heard Tom head out of the room he said, "Thanks, Tom."

Tom turned, with a concerned look on his face, knowing that Charlie couldn't see him, "You're welcome. Get some sleep you have a long trip ahead of you."

Back Home Again in Old Kentucky

Marie had struggled with the sporadic communications from Tom. She had seen the newscasts from the area and was so concerned about Charlie and Tom she could barely eat. They had sent her one letter before the TET offensive had begun, and she had waited a month before she heard from either of them again. It was a difficult month. She had missed a period and had thought she might be pregnant. She kept the speculation to herself. Thankfully when the next month rolled around, her monthly cycle came on time.

In that month, she had time to really think about what a full relationship with Tom would mean and how her life would change if they were to marry and have children.

Marie stopped what she was doing when the news came over the radio about the assassination of Martin Luther King, Jr. She had no one to talk to about it and didn't know what it would mean to the Civil Rights Movement, which was still being chewed about in the news. Walter Cronkite, one of the most respected journalists of the day, speculated that his death might spark more riots. He was proven correct as riots in Baltimore, Kansas City, Boston, Chicago, Detroit, and Washington, DC occurred throughout the summer.

When Charlie's parents got word of Charlie's injuries, they headed to DC where they stayed in Charlie's apartment for the next two and a half months until he was dismissed, then they traveled back home to Lexington.

Marie knocked, then opened the door to the White's kitchen. "Yoohoo," she yelled as she shut the door behind her.

"In here, Honey," Sandra White answered.

Marie headed into the living room that was nearly as much home as her own was. "Hi, Sandy. Is Charlie up to seeing me?"

Sandra gave her a sad smile. "I don't know, Marie. He didn't say much on the way home. He just kept looking out the window. He hasn't said much since we got home yesterday. He was given an eye patch to wear for a while so his eyes will rest for as long as they can. He is supposed to have the patch off for an hour, then on for two hours. That is the routine for a week, then he will go to two hours on and two hours off. The next week, he would be three hours off and two hours on, and so on. The doctors want to see him again in a month. I think he is afraid they will muster him out of the service on a health discharge. Between you and me, I would be fine if he didn't go back to that damned Hell hole, but it would destroy him."

Marie nodded, thinking about the times she had listened to Charlie and Tom discuss their jobs. They were dedicated soldiers. They believed they could make a difference and therefore made it their life's choice of work. She knew how she felt about teaching. She would be devastated if something happened to keep her from doing what she felt she had been born to do. "I think I will go ahead up and pop in anyway. Maybe he will be glad enough to see me that he will talk some. He can't keep things bottled up. That won't be good at all."

Sandra White nodded and gave her a smile then went back to the brightly colored afghan she was crocheting.

"Hey there, Charlie?" Marie gave a couple of knocks as she then turned the knob and began to open the door. "Are you decent?"

"Marie? Wait a minute. Don't want you to see my junk."

Marie chuckled and laughed, stopping her entrance. "Oh, darn. I was hoping to get a peek."

"I know a big guy serving his country in Vietnam who would whip my ass if he thought I showed you my equipment," Charlie laughed back.

"Hmmm... now that I think about that big guy, you are probably right. Hurry up. I want a hug."

"Okay, come on in."

Marie bounded in and gave Charlie a big hug before he sat back down on the bed, readjusting his pajamas and leaning back on the pillows before pulling up the sheet over his feet and up to his waist. He had moved over to make room for Marie to sit on the bed too so they could talk.

"How are you, really?" she asked in a soft voice, full of concern.

He took her hand and held it, massaging it as he answered. "I am okay, physically. I will get better. The sight problem is getting

better. Mentally, Mare, I am fucked up. I
keep waking up with dreams of the explosion.
I don't remember much of it. I remember
hearing the plane and running to save the little
girls. That's it."

"Have you ever considered that is all
you are supposed to remember? What good
would it do you to remember more about the
whole thing? Really. Think about it. Would
anything be changed? You tried to protect
someone from danger. You did protect them.
You got injured and you are healing. The idea
that you and Tom are in harm's way daily
makes me ill. I think about it and I get sick at
my stomach. So, I try to think differently and
realize that you are trained for what you do. I
trust neither of you to do something foolish
that would cause harm to yourself or others. I
put my trust in God, Charlie, to protect you
and Tom."

"Marie, we had no idea what we were
going to be seeing over there. I mean, I would
still be there, but they should have prepared
us better.   They should have prepared us
better," he repeated.

"Hey, how is Tom?" She tried to appear
a bit nonchalant as she asked the question,

but she failed. Charlie could see the desperate look in her eyes as she asked about the man she loved.

Looking her right in the eye he told her, "When I left, he told me to tell you he had something for you when he next sees you. Now, he didn't say what it was, but I thought of a few things he might want to give you."

Marie laughed at the way Charlie grinned at her as he delivered that line and smacked his uninjured arm. "You are so bad!!"

The two broke out laughing. "Want to play some cards?" she asked, changing the subject.

"Any time, penny a point?"

"You are on!" she said as she got off the bed and went over to get the deck of cards off his desk and begin an afternoon of fun.

Another Kennedy Gone

Charlie and Marie fell into an easy routine. Playing cards nightly, sometimes with one of their sets of parents but often alone, the two talked often about Tom. Other evenings, they prepared dinner for their parents and all ate together. When Marie was with her roommates at their apartment in Cincinnati, Charlie would stay with them for a few days at a time.

It was at breakfast that they heard the news that Robert Kennedy had been killed the evening before as he exited a hotel through the kitchen after delivering a speech at a hotel in Los Angeles. Tragedy seemed to follow the Kennedy family and had for years. The nation once more mourned. The assassination of John Kennedy in 1963 then earlier in 1968 the assassination of Martin Luther King, now this. The friends discussed how much more the country could take of this kind of violence and hate. They came up with no answers but mourned together as they considered the state of the world.

About the only good news they were able to focus on were the Paris Peace talks.

North Vietnam and the United States were engaged in talks to see if any kind of resolution could be made in the war. South Vietnam had yet to agree to the talks, so it was an extremely slow process.

Charlie continued to heal and Marie continued to listen. It took its toll on her because she absorbed so much of the pain. Her faith kept her grounded and Charlie came dangerously close to falling in love with her himself during those troubling times.

"Marie," he said one evening. "How serious are things between you and Tom from your side of the fence?"

Marie's face took on a glow as she began talking about Tom. "He is the rest of me," she replied. "I am complete, by myself, don't get me wrong," she began explaining. "I think we are all complete just as we are. Then, one day, if we are lucky, we meet someone who just makes us more than we ever thought we could be. They fill up all of the parts of ourselves that are empty. They complete us. Do you know what I mean?"

"No," Charlie replied. "I have never had that kind of intensity in a relationship."

"Oh, I think you can have good relationships without that, but when you get that in addition, it is miraculous. I would never have guessed it if I wasn't experiencing it myself. I know there are problems in this country because I have a light skin and Tom has a darker skin, but I think, speaking for myself, what we have is worth fighting for. I hope Tom feels that way. We did not really have a lot of time to sort through those things, you know?"

Marie paused while she saw Charlie thinking over what she had said, then she continued. "You know, at one time my ancestors, the Irish, came over to this country and were treated as badly as people in the black treated slaves. We were not bought and sold in exactly the same way. We weren't shackled and whipped, but we were slaves. We wanted to come to the United States and our passage was bought for a certain number of years. We were indentured to those people and we agreed to work for a certain number of years to pay that debt off. Now, we agreed to work for about twice the length of time that would have reflected the value of those tickets, but we didn't know that. We were expecting people to treat us fairly and justly. We were wrong, they didn't. When we were nearing the end of our indentured time, there were many instances where situations were constructed that added time to our term of indenture. Oh, Charlie, we were slaves too but those 'employers' would be sympathetic and tell us that they knew we had it bad, but they would also tell us, 'at least you are not black.'"

She continued, "I know the problems. My classroom is integrated. I see the looks that some of the kids give the others. I hear some of the comments of parents when we have activities. I see the looks that some of my friends give a mixed couple and know if they were to see me even sit and share a soda with Tom I could no longer count them as a friend." Then she dropped her voice, "And I know what would happen if I were to bring him to dinner. It wouldn't be resolved as easily as Katharine Hepburn solved it either. It would rip me apart, but I would do it because that is how much I love Tom."

"Well, kiddo, sounds like you have done a lot of thinking about this. You know I have your back on this, don'tcha?"

She gave a shy look over at Charlie. "Does Tom ever talk about me?"

"Nope., he said. "He doesn't have time to talk about you. He holds your picture and talks TO YOU. It is just sad and sorry how much that guy loves you, Marie," he chuckled. "I told him he had just better treat you right or he will have to deal with me, but I don't think that will ever happen."

Marie brightened as they began discussing Tom. Charlie had met his parents and gave his description of what they were like to her.She asked him if he thought they would accept her if they found out the two of them were together.

"I think they would. Tom has a couple of cousins who are in mixed marriages and they are working out. One is in Virginia and one is in New York. Shoot, I have a couple of other cousins who are not in a mixed marriage, who are both white as the driven snow and they are having all kinds of problems. I don't think it has anything to do with skin color. I think it has more to do with the values you live by every day and how attune you are to your partner. If you have basic differences on how you approach life, you may stay married, but I don't think it will be very happy."

"You are probably right," she agreed. "I have no idea how Tom spends his money or what he wants in life beyond a military career. How does he feel about his wife working after children are born? There are so very many things that couples need to discuss. This war is causing things to shrink down. We meet someone and fall in love then get married before we really know them."

"Do you ever know anyone until you live with them, Marie? And, even when you are living with then, we somehow think that we can change them when we are married."

"Charlie, that makes no sense. If you fall in love with the person, the real person, the deep - who they are - person, why would you ever want them to change?"

"Hahaha… when you say it like that, it sounds preposterous, but it does happen and often."

Charlie realized that he was lucky to have the kind of relationship he had with Marie. She would always be his best friend, even better than Tom. He would never do anything to lose that, but there was just a little corner of his heart that was broken when he realized what he would never have with her.

Goodbye, Charlie

Charlie had gone back and forth between Kentucky and Washington, DC for most of the summer. He was still assigned to the base at Quantico. It was in the middle of August that he received his orders. He would be sent back to finish the terms of his original deployment. He would be back in the arena with Tom. Charlie had been privy to some of the military communications that had been received from Saigon and surrounding areas like Xuan Loc. He knew that peace talks were stalled. The South Vietnamese refused to make certain concessions and although the United States delegates to the Peace talks in Paris had tried to change their minds, it hadn't happened yet.

Charlie had been feeling much better over the summer, thanks to all of his conversations with Marie. She had an outlook that was contagious and had helped Charlie look at things a bit differently. He wanted to get back to his men, but this deployment was much different than the first one, where he and Tom had met. It had been characterized by more discovery and more naivete. They now knew the belly of the beast.

There were tears in Marie's eyes as she hugged Charlie goodbye. She had made the trip with him and his parents to the Cincinnati airport to see him off. She had sent a very private letter to Tom with him. There were things she had to tell him that she didn't want to take the risk of landing in the hands of anyone but Tom. She kept her hug on Charlie and was reluctant to let go. He had been her lifeline to Tom for the last three months and it was like letting go of Tom.

"Tell, him, ..." she sobbed but could not finish as she rested her head on his chest

Charlie simply nodded and removed her arms from around his waist. "I will, but you realize he already knows. You two have a connection that crosses the oceans. What you are feeling, I can guarantee he is feeling too. I know the talks I have had with him and the ones I have had with you. Marie, they are the same conversations. You have nothing to worry about. He saved my life when I was in the hospital. He brought me out of depression. I would lay down my life for that guy. Don't you worry. We will get through this and get back here. Talks can't stay stalled much longer. It will be okay." He kissed her temple, then her cheek as he gave her one last hug before he went to his parents and gave them hugs and kisses. With one look back at the three of them, he went through the doorway to begin his journey back to Saigon.

Back in Hell

If Charlie thought things were going to be better, he was mistaken. Even though there were peace talks going on in Paris, you would never have known it on the ground in Vietnam. There was fighting on all fronts in all areas. It was rare to have a day where there wasn't some kind of skirmish that Tom and Charlie had to investigate. Tom had become very adapt at the Vietnamese language, so he was able to get information that others were unable to understand.

Charlie thought he would be able to go back in at the level he left. That was not to be the case. The battalion had evolved during his absence.

"Pull the M16 inventory and compare it to the M14 numbers," the sergeant on duty said.

"There should be a convenience ratio there. Why do we need to pull them, Soldier?" Charlie asked.

"Sir, there have been rifles going missing and the Captain wants everything inventoried, Sir," replied the sergeant.

"Fair enough," said Charlie. "Now, then, what's next?"

"There are Colt M1911, .45ACP handguns, M79 Grenade launchers, M60 machine guns, and a few MA2 .50 caliber machine guns. Cap says to get them all inventoried and locked down before nightfall. Do you want me to call some other guys in here to help?"

"Nah, I think we can do it, Sarge."

The two men counted and sorted. After the job was done, they found that they were seventy guns short. A bewildered Charlie asked, "How the hell did that many guns go missing? We need to inventory the barracks and the men to make sure they aren't there. Don't we keep a running list of who gets issued what guns?"

"Sure do, Sir. There should be," he paused, looking at the clipboard with several papers attached to it, "Let's see. Eight hundred seventy-three guns in this company. Each company will have different stats and different counts. If ours is off by this much, their count is probably off also. Either the men are getting sloppy, or someone is filching the guns after hours. I have an idea."

"What's that, soldier?"

"Why don't we inventory the ammo for those guns? We know how many rounds we have per gun. If the ammo count is okay, we just have sloppy housekeeping. If the ammo is gone too, then we have theft. It could be villagers or it could be our own guys selling off weapons on the side. Either way, we need to know."

"Sounds good." Charlie looked at his watch. It was about time to hang it up for the day, but he would feel better if they got the job done sooner rather than later. If he had evidence to take to Tom, it would give them more time to come up with a solution to the problem, whichever it was.

The men went to the ammo cabinet and determined that it appeared to be sloppy housekeeping, except for the M79 Grenade Launchers. The ammo for those had all but disappeared. Twelve launchers were gone and most of the corresponding ammo. If the men needed to arm those, they were shit out of luck with no more ammo than this at their disposal. Tom would have to be informed of the data they had collected.

"That's it!!?? That is all the ammo for the M79 available? How in the fuck did that happen?"

"Don't know, Sir. The Lieutenant here and I counted the guns like you asked us to. There were some missing but we didn't know if they had been stolen or if the guys had just been sloppy. I thought the only way we could figure it out would be to inventory the ammo."

"That was good thinking, Sarge," Tom said as he calmed down. At least now they knew what was missing and how much was missing. The only thing they didn't know was why it was missing. The why disturbed him on any level. He had a thief, either local or Cong. Or, he had an incredibly inept inventory clerk. Either way, there was not much he could do. If the thief was local, it could be one of his men looking to sell on the black market and cash in on government property. This could be a disaster in the making, and it could cost some of his men their lives if some of the scenarios played out.

Tom complimented them on their thoroughness and they went back to the barracks. Tom had been moved while Charlie was gone. He was billeted with the other officers, a marine perk unavailable to a man until he reached the office of Captain. Tom felt like the distance imposed by their housing caused his his friendship with Charlie to wane. They also had the precarious position of having Charlie serve under Tom. There was a no fraternizing rule, but it didn't apply since there was no suggestion that either one was undermining themselves by their friendship. It was also a moot point since they were both officially officers, just at different pay scales.

There were still battles all over Vietnam. Because of its proximity to Saigon, the area around Xuan Loc was less volatile than other areas of the country. It was at the end of October when President Johnson announced a total halt to the bombing of North Vietnam. After months of stalling, the South Vietnamese finally stepped up to the negotiation table at the end of November.

There were prayers said all over the world that there would be an end to this fighting.

One Down and Two to Go

Tom and Charlie celebrated the New Year with a trip to Saigon. They had saved their leave so they could visit the city now that most fighting had stopped. While in the city, they went to a dining establishment that specialized in some of the wines that Vietnam was known for. They even imbibed some Snake wine, which is created a couple of ways. Often a venomous snake is simply steeped in a variety of rice wine for several days then poured off to be bottled. Another way is to dissolve the venom of the snake in the wine where it is neutralized by the ethanol in the alcohol. They agreed it was a unique experience and not one they were likely to repeat, but they could lay claim to having done it.

Neither Tom nor Charlie usually over indulged when they drank, but that night they did. It was only in the morning that they regretted their actions from the night before.

"Did we really get up in that nightclub and sing?" Charlie asked.

"We didn't," Tom laughed. "You did."

"Oh," Charlie said as he held his head, "don't laugh so loud."

The two men took some headache powder and drank a lot of water then went back to bed to get some more sleep. They both hoped they woke up the next time feeling much better.

As January commenced, the war developed a different flavor. Lyndon Johnson would soon be out of the office of President and Richard Nixon would be inaugurated. While there were peace talks going on, and a supposed end to the bombing, there was still a lot of fighting going on.

On January 22, 1969 the 9th Marine regiment launched a campaign, Operation Dewey Canyon, that swept through the Da Krong Valleys of South Vietnam in an effort to rid the region of the North Vietnamese troops. It was a fifty-six day effort that was considered a tactical win but in actuality did little to eliminate the North Vietnamese from the area.

Tom had been studying the strategies of war and had offered ideas that had been used by those who were higher in rank and had proved to be very successful. He had been advised that another promotion would be on the fast track once they got back to the States.

"How the fuck can we say this war is winding down?" Tom asked Charlie one day when they were walking to the hospital to check on some of their men that had been ambushed a couple of days ago.

"I don't know," said Charlie. "I just don't know."

It was March of 1969. The parties were talking peace, but there had been recent killings by the North Vietnamese, and President Nixon had threatened to renew bombing of the North.

The troops in Vietnam were at an all-time high of half a million and there had been as many people killed to date as had been killed in the Korean War. The summer and fall of 1969 were among some of the worst in Vietnam from a psychological standpoint. The men heard of renewed peace talks but that always seemed to be followed by renewed bombings.

At the same time, in September, charges were brought against William Calley for his duplicity in the My Lai incident where over three hundred civilians including children were murdered in a "search and destroy" mission.

The word came down early in October that the command post was going to be dismantled in Xuan Loc. The men were being sent back to Saigon and would be among some of the first to be sent back home. The morale was higher than it had been for months. It was when they were headed back that the men were attacked by a group of Viet Cong that had evaded capture. The truck Tom was riding in was blown off the road, and he was thrown to the side before it exploded. Charlie was in one of the other trucks further behind when the fireball exploded. He ordered the truck to stop, and he took off running to see what had happened.

He had the men check for survivors of the blast. As he walked back to the truck, not realizing it was Tom's vehicle that had blown, he noticed the heap alongside the road. As he investigated, he saw that it was Tom then called the medics to come and help him.

"You sure go to great lengths to get to spend some time with the cute nurses, but what is Marie going to say?" Charlie asked Tom as he walked into the hospital area.

"Shut the fuck up and get out of here," Tom barked at his best friend.

"Nope," said Charlie as he mimicked the words that Tom had said to him over a year ago. "Not going to happen that way. You are headed home. You are going to be spending Thanksgiving and Christmas in the States this year. Your leg is healing. You have been feeling sorry for yourself for a month now. You almost lost that fucking leg, but you didn't. Yeah, you will have some scars for life, but you have your leg and you can walk. You have a woman waiting for you at home. I got a private message off to her when I got in touch with your folks. She has to be beside herself. She has no one to talk to about the two of you. Man up and get your ass out of that bed, do your rehab, take the leave and then get yourself back here asap so we can get this fucking deployment out of the way."

Marie and Shelly

When Marie heard the news about Tom, she had to take a day off. She was in no shape to go to school and try to maintain any semblance of professionalism. She would have been a basket case if she had tried to teach that day. She hadn't even gotten dressed. Instead, she roamed around the apartment in her pajamas all day. She had tried to eat an egg and couldn't keep that down. She finally got some pudding to stay down. She had slept for the larger part of the day. Sleep was the only way she could keep from crying but the dreams that woke her were not much better.

Shelly came rushing in the door. "Oh, Marie. You missed the excitement today. Gina Gilbert had a meltdown. Her mother had to come and get her, and she was not a happy camper. I bet Gina got her little butt blistered when they got home. Woohee. I would not want to be that little girl." She caught her breath then noticed Marie's distress. She went over and got down on her knees in front of Marie, putting her hand on Marie's shoulder. "What's wrong, Honey?"

Marie was sniffing so hard she could barely talk. "It is just this war. Someone special over there... He was injured and is on his way back to the states for a while. He will be in Washington, DC and I want to go see him."

"Well, then what's the problem? Go visit him. Easy, peasy."

"My parents don't know about him. I just started seeing him and then he went to Vietnam. I have been writing to him for a couple of years but he hasn't been home so the subject just hasn't come up with them," she sniffed.

'Well, then just make up a friend you are going to visit. I mean, as long as you are home for Christmas Day, you are here in Cincinnati and they are in Lexington. They don't know what you do any other day of the week. Why would this be different? Maybe you can just kind of give them the idea that you are going there with friends for a mini vacation during your break."

"Oh," Marie said. "I have always played it pretty straight with them. I don't want to start lying to them now, not this late in the game."

"I am sure you will think of something, now dish me the news. Who is this guy, and did you meet him when you went out to that ball with Charlie? Wait! It isn't Charlie is it???"

"No!" Marie laughed. "It would be easier if it were Charlie. That they would approve of, this guy they wouldn't."

"What's wrong with him?"

""Nothing, absolutely nothing. He and I knew after only a few hours that we had something special. We just haven't had time for it to develop. I think my parents will flip if they think I am in love with someone I barely know." Marie covered her story with Shelly. She knew that Shelly had a friend who had dated a black man and she had not been comfortable with that relationship when she talked about that. Marie thought their friendship was strong enough to survive any difficulties, but she wasn't ready to take that step quite yet.

Shelly got up and went to change clothes. She came back in and asked Marie if an oven casserole would be okay for supper. Marie was certain she wouldn't be hungry and if she were, she knew that Shelly's casserole would be wonderful.

As Marie and Shelly were eating their dinner and discussing some of the events of the day, Tabitha burst in the door. "Well, I am only back long enough to shower and change. I just got switched to a London-Barcelona flight for a three month sting. I will be in Europe over Christmas and into the New Year!! Can you believe it?"

The girls were all in a state of excitement. Tabitha worked as a stewardess for American Airlines and was often out of town but they all had a great time when she had time off. They would miss their friend but knew it would be a great experience for her.

"I will be staying in the AmAir facility in London and that will be my home base. I make the trip, do a turnaround that day and should be spending all my nights in London. Oh, my gosh. Can you believe it?! Some of the gals over there have been there so long they have their own apartments--or should I say 'flats'--and know their way around the best pubs and theatres. Ohhhh...." She began jumping up and down at the thought of seeing other parts of the world.

"That means we will have to wait and celebrate the holidays when I get back. You will have to leave the tree up."

Marie and Shelly looked at each other then remarked, "Girl, you are crazy if you think we are going to leave a tree up until the middle of February. We might leave that little ceramic one out, but not the big silver one."

"Well, okay then. Just be that way. I will remember that when I do my Christmas shopping at Harrod's."

The girls all laughed. Knowing Tabitha's love of shopping, there would be no way that would happen.

Tabitha had Marie and Shelly pack up as many of her clothes as she could in the two bags she was allowed to take. She had her personal bag packed quickly after she showered and dressed.

"Well," she said as she stalled on her way out the door. "I was looking forward to this but now, I am kind of scared," she confessed.

"Scared???? You???" Marie said, surprised at the idea. "You are one of the bravest people I know. You are always ready for that next great adventure."

"Yeah, but this is just a little different. I am going to miss you guys."

"Aw…" said Shelly. "We are going to miss you too, but that time is going to fly by and you will be back before you know it unless you meet a good looking Brit who sweeps you off your feet."

"One can live and hope," Tabitha sighed.

They heard the cab honk and all hugged once more before Tabitha turned and left.

Shelly closed the door and both girls looked around at the space. "It already feels strange to have Tabitha gone, doesn't it?"

"Yes," said Marie. "She has such a presence, such energy. Sure leaves a space."

The two finished their portions of dinner, cleared the dishes, and turned on the television to watch what was happening in the world besides the war.

Settling In

Tom had gotten himself set in the officer's quarters. He had called his parents who were on their way to visit. He had healed enough that he had not had to be admitted to Walter Reed. He was just to come in daily for the first week, then every other day, then he would be given a thirty day leave beginning about December 5th. He had plans for that leave. Plans that included getting married.

Tom's parents were able to stay in Washington, DC for a couple of weeks while he was tied to the hospital. They all then went home for Thanksgiving. Tom had a serious discussion with his parents about his plans, yet didn't tell them he would be marrying the girl, only that he would be proposing. He wasn't sure they would approve of him marrying her since they had not really known each other very long. It was a risk he was willing to take.

The first weekend in December, Tom finally called Marie to let her know that he was going to be on leave for thirty days and that he wanted to visit her in Cincinnati. He had let his parents know that if there was a way he could come to visit then he would, but he really wanted to spend additional time with Marie to get to know her better. He thought some additional time would let them determine whether their feelings were real or whether their attraction had been born of insecurities about the state of the world.

After hearing from Tom, Marie realized that she had to tell Shelly about him. He would be staying with them, in Marie's room, for a few weeks and Marie hoped it would not be the end of her friendship with Shelly.

"He's what?" Shelly said, when she and Marie talked that evening.

"He's a Captain in the Marines who was stationed near Saigon. He was injured and sent home to recuperate before he leaves to go back to the war."

"Yeah, I got that part," said Shelly impatiently. " What was the other part you tried to sneak by me?"

"I said that he happens to also be black."

"Marie, do you realize the problems you will have?"

"I know my parents will probably be upset when they find out, but I will deal with that when it happens. I just want to know if your are okay with it."

"Yeah, why wouldn't I be?"

"I remember your friend Lindsey had a black boyfriend, and you didn't seem comfortable with it."

"I wasn't comfortable with it because he was an asshole. Your guy isn't an asshole, is he?

Marie laughed at the very idea. "No, not at all. I think you will like him."

"Well, that remains to be seen. Is he going to be staying here?"

"If you don't mind, I will let him stay in my room."

Shelly's eyes widened. "Are you sure? I mean, are you really that sure?"

"Yes, I am really that sure."

Shelly went over and hugged her friend. "You just be careful who you tell about this. There are some of the teachers at school who are very narrow-minded about relationships like this, ya know? I can see a couple of the jealous old biddies who would try to make trouble for you."

"I hadn't thought of that."

"Yeah, well, you need to be thinking about that kind of thing if you are going to be involved with someone, anyone, of another race. It shouldn't be a problem, but it is for a lot of people."

Reunion Weekend

After the plane had stopped in Cincinnati, Tom took his bag down from the overhead compartment and wondered what would happen after he deboarded. He had Marie's address and was not sure whether she would come to meet him at the airport. Giving her a hug and kiss if he saw there to greet him was not debatable. Anyone who saw their greeting would know instantly that she was his woman. The thought of her in his arms caused his groin to jerk.

Marie was standing there waiting. As people began to leave the plane, she craned her neck to get the first glimpse of Tom. They had not seen each other for two years, and she was so excited to see him and fly into his arms. She had thought about how public this would be. If she rushed into his arms, people would stare. Did she care? She decided that her nervousness stemmed from the fact they had not seen each other in so long and nothing else. She had spent the last two years reconciling how people would react, and she was literally tired of trying to figure out what bothered other people.

Tom looked out and saw Marie looking straight his way with the most amazing smile on her face. She began running toward him with her arms open. He scooped her up, holding her tightly, kissing her as though she was the very elixir of life. "Oh, Tom," she said before their lips met. Tom lowered her slowly as the kiss continued. He remembered where they were and eased away from her. His hands slid out from around her waist but grabbed her hand and held it.

"Marie, you are more beautiful than I remember," He could not keep himself from slipping his arm around her shoulder and pulling her toward him in a big hug. Her arm slid up and around his shoulder and their lips met again. They were oblivious to the looks they received. Some recognized and celebrated their reunion and some looked rather disgusted. The two didn't care. They were together again.

After the initial warm greeting, Tom slung his duffel over his shoulder and they headed out holding hands. Marie had her silver Pontiac Grand Prix backed out of the parking lot and on her way to the apartment in record time. "My roommate, Shelly, isn't real sure about this. She has no problem as long as you aren't an asshole. You aren't, are you?"

"I try not to be unless you are a soldier incapable of following the smallest orders," he replied with a smile.

"Well, then, alrighty. I guess we are good to go."

They pulled into the parking lot and Marie found her spot. She and Tom were walking toward the door when Mrs. Brown from next door arrived home also.

"Hello, Marie," she said as she looked curiously at Tom.

Marie knew she was nosy, but seemed rather harmless. "This is my friend, Captain Martin, home on leave from Vietnam."

Mrs. Brown tensed up. "Well, I would think he would choose to stay with his Negro friends and visit. Why is he here?"

Marie kept her temper as she answered, "He is here because we are friends, and we hope to spend more time getting to know each other. This is my boyfriend, Mrs. Brown."

The look of horror would have amused them both if it had not been so genuine. "You can't be serious, Marie. I thought you were a nice girl. You have young children in your care every day. What would their parents think if they knew you had a Negro boyfriend, and that he was staying in your apartment, doing God knows what the two of you. And Shelly is there too, that just isn't right."

"Mrs. Brown, I like to think I am a nice girl. I am a nice neighbor to you. Once a week you come over here and have dinner with Shelly and me. This week, come over and have dinner with Shelly, Tom, and me. You will see what my friend is like. After you do that, then you can make a judgement that is more fair. Okay?"

She considered it for a moment, "Okay, I guess you might be right." She gave a terse smile to the couple, let herself in her apartment, and quickly closed the door. The two heard her click the lock and slide the chain into the additional security on the door as if she were afraid they would come in and do her bodily harm.

Tom shrugged. "Get used to it, Marie. This is what goes with the territory. I get attitude like that all the time. You need to know what you are getting into if we continue to see each other."

Marie had unlocked the door and they had gone in. She closed the door, put her purse on the table, and he got rid of the duffel. They were in each other's arms instantly. After they had explored each other's mouths, she said, "Being with you is not even a consideration. I will be yours until the day I die and beyond. I don't care what is thrown at us. The most serious consideration I have is how my parents will deal with this."

"You haven't mentioned me?"

"No. I haven't. I have started to several times, but it just never seemed right. They are kind of inconsistent."

"How so?" he questioned.

"They say they believe in the integration of schools, but they ask questions about some of my black students in a way that says they really feel like blacks are not as good as we are."

"We?"

"See, I do it too. White, we... Oh, Tom. I don't feel like that inside. I just don't know the right words. I feel like when I talk, it comes out wrong."

"Baby, I hear you. It will take time for attitudes to change. I just don't want you caught in the trample while it happens."

"It will only defeat us if we allow it to. When my parents find out about us, we will weather any storm together."

Tom nuzzled into her neck and mumbled. "Right now I want you to tell me that your roommate will not be home for at least three hours."

"Shelly is spending the weekend at friends' of ours and promised that she will not be home until 6 pm on Sunday evening. The place is ours."

"Thank you, Lord," Tom said as his eyes raised to the heavens and he bent down and swooped Marie in his arms.

She pointed down the hall, "Door on the left."

He placed her down and they both began undressing each other. The took the task slowly, finally standing in front of each other in only their underwear. Marie blushed as Tom's eyes slowly began at her feet and looked up, stopping at the panties, noting the wet spot in the light blue crotch where her body was responding to his. His hard cock jumped, and he reached down to stroke it.

Marie took her lip in her mouth and bit down with her upper teeth as she noted his body's response. She started to step toward him and touch his hard manhood, but he put his hand out to stop her. "No. I want to see you, all of you, first."

She stepped back as he finished his perusal of her body. She then stepped forward to grab his hand and pull him toward the bed. She turned around and knew that he was enjoying the view. When she got to the bed, she reached around and unhooked her bra, letting it drop from her shoulders before she took it off. She then put her thumbs in the waistband of her panties and took them all the way down to her ankles before stepping out of them. She heard Tom's intake of breath as she kicked them off her feet and turned around to face him.

He pumped his hard on before following her into the bed. She laid on her stomach, and he crawled over enough to begin kissing her shoulders as his hand found its way down to her cheeks and began massaging them. She heard a moan but she was unaware of whose lips it came from. She rolled to her side and the two met in an intense hug. It was not going to last long this time, and maybe not the next time. They were so hot for each other that after one swipe of Tom's hand to her pussy to see if she was slick enough for him, he entered her with one deep thrust.

Marie gasped as Tom entered her and they began meeting each other thrust for thrust. The build up and release was quick for both of them, and they laid in each other's arms to rest before they continued what was going to be a long, long evening.

Marie woke up alone. She smelled fresh coffee and breakfast cooking. She quickly showered and washed her hair before donning a nightshirt and joining Tom in the kitchen.

"Ah, there you are. Coffee?" he asked.

As he poured coffee for them both, she asked, "Do you take cream and sugar in your coffee?"

Tom looked over at her as he picked up the cups to take them to the table. He leaned down and kissed her on the forehead as she sat down. "You are the cream in my coffee, love."

The couple laughed and sipped their coffee. "Jeez Marie. I had just settled down, and you come in here and I am hard again."

Marie looked down at his briefs, and as she watched, he began to get harder. "See what just the idea of having you in my arms and me in your pussy does to me?

"Well, then, I guess we need to do something about that. Turn off the stove and come with me."

"That is exactly what I am hoping to do," he mumbled as he turned the burners off and put the pans over to the side on the counter.

The two explored every inch of each other as they made love not once, but twice before getting up to shower again. It was nearly noon and the fillings for the omelettes that Tom had been fixing were still sitting, just waiting to be warmed up before adding the eggs. He turned the oven back on, let it preheat, then pushed the biscuits in while he poured some orange juice and fixed the omelettes. While they ate the delicious meal, they discussed what they would be doing for the rest of the day.

"I think, since it is noon already, we could just hang out here for the day. You just came off a flight, you haven't had much rest, and you can't afford to get sick while you are continuing to heal." Tom couldn't disagree with her, so they finished their late breakfast, cleaned up the dishes, and made their way to the living room couch where they watched a Saturday afternoon movie wrapped in each other's arms.

Tom woke up with Marie's head leaned back on his shoulder and his arms around her just like they had been sitting while watching television before they had both dozed off. It was already beginning to get dark. He didn't want to wake her up, but when he moved, her eyes fluttered open and she stretched, arching her back and pushing her full breasts out. His hands seemed to have a mind of their own as he reached to take her breasts in his hands and rub her nipples with his thumbs.

"Mmm. Tom. That feels good, but I am so tired." She sank into him, resting her back against his chest as he continued rubbing her breasts, massaging them, then bending down to kiss her neck.

"Okay, mister," she said as she leaned up and away from him. "You are seriously getting me hot again. Come on. Let's go to bed. I have to have you inside me. Now."

"I am certainly not going to begin arguing with you as soon as we get back together," he said as they both got up and went into the bedroom.

Tom and Marie had finely tuned movements. It was as though they had done this dance thousands of times. They both knew where to put their hands, their mouths, and their bodies to give the other partner the most satisfaction that could be had from the experience.

Meeting the Sinclairs

The next few days were easy ones. Marie and Shelly still had a week to go before the school break. Shelly had approved of Tom right at the start, but she was still a bit concerned about how some of the other teachers in the building would take it when they found out Marie was dating a black man. That would not be her problem, so she felt that the best she could do was be a friend when Marie needed one.

"Tom," Marie began.

"What?" he replied. He could tell by the tenor of her voice that there was something troubling her.

"Have you let Charlie's parents know you will be staying with them on Christmas?"

"Yes, I have. I already told them that Charlie had gotten in touch with you and you would be picking me up at the airport and bringing me there with you. I thought that would take any responsibility off of your shoulders for trying to tell your parents why you were driving up the street with a black man in your car." He slipped his arms around her waist and pulled her close then kissed her temple. "We will be okay."

"Oh," she said, with a sigh of relief. "I had been trying to figure out what to tell them. Thank you." She placed her hand on his strong bicep as she put her head on his shoulder. He felt so safe. Why couldn't life be simple? "I do want you to meet my parents while you are at Charlie's. We usually all get together on Christmas Eve. The families traditionally buy each other one of the new games that have come out that year, then we play them, and have treats and mulled wine that evening. It used to be a bit different when Charlie and I were younger, but this is what we have worked in to."

"Sounds like a good time. I know Charlie's parents like me, so maybe it will work out more easily than you think."

"I hope so. I mean, my parents won't be rude to you. They just may be a bit standoffish."

Tom wasn't concerned. He and Marie had discussed their future enough that he was fairly certain she would be open to marrying him before he left to go back to Vietnam. They could get their license and get married in

Richmond the same day. No waiting and no blood test. The plans were that she would tell her folks that she was going to spend New Year's with friends and leave it for them to assume that she would still be in Cincinnati. She would not volunteer information, but she had told him that she would not lie to her parents if they had any reason to ask her specific questions.

Marie drove into the driveway and exclaimed, "Oh, dear."

Tom looked up and saw two men playing basketball in the large turnaround area that both garages shared. "Let me guess, your dad?"

"Yep. Into the belly of the tiger." She turned off the key then they both got out of the car.

"That is seven points to four points," Brian Sinclair shouted as Wes Johnson took the ball to the side to bring it back into play.

"Well, enjoy yourself, Brian. I am going to trim that lead."

"Riiiight. We are only playing to ten, remember?"

Wes dodged to the side and slipped around Brian to jump up and score. "Five to seven now."

Brian went to the side, brought the ball in, and Wes quickly stole it and tipped it up to the basket for another point. "Six to seven," he responded.

Marie wanted her dad to be in a good mood so she thought now, while he was ahead, would be a good time to interrupt them.

"Hi, Wes," she acknowledged the friend as she went over to her dad and he hugged her lightly.

"I'm sweaty honey, You don't want to get all stinky, do ya?"

Marie laughed. "You aren't that sweaty, and yes, I want to hug you even if that means getting stinky."

In the meantime, Tom had gone over to Wes and was shaking his hand when he turned to introduce Charlie's friend to Brian Sinclair.

"Brian, this is Charlie's best friend, besides Marie, Thomas Martin. Captain Thomas Martin."

Brian extended his hand. "Good to meet you," he said as they shook hands.

"The pleasure is mine, Sir," Tom responded.

"Brian, I will let you get by with this win. I need to get this guy in to give Sandy a hug from Charlie." He put his hand on Tom's shoulder. "I am sure glad you could be here, Son. We are missing Charlie like the dickens. It was so kind of your parents to share you. You will be with them later, won't you?"

"That's the plan, Sir," He then turned and spoke to Marie. "Thanks for picking me up at the airport and bringing me here. I appreciate it greatly."

"It was my pleasure, Tom. I am sure we will have a chance to visit more in the next two or three days. As a matter of fact, you can certainly ride back to Indy with me and I will be happy to drop you off for you to go to your parents'."

"Thanks. We will see if our times coordinate. See you folks later," he gave a nod as he picked up his duffel and followed Wes into the Johnson's home.

"Seems like a nice guy, for a Negro," Brian said as he put the basketball on the bench outside the kitchen door and opened it up for Marie to go in. "I'll get your bags in a minute. I know your mom is wanting to see you."

Linda Sinclair was getting a pan of brownies out of the oven as the two came in. "Look what the cat dragged in."

Linda looked up and smiled, setting the pan on the stove and coming over to hug Marie, then she stepped back. "Something looks different about you."

About that time, Black Jack, the cat, rubbed up against Marie's ankles and gave her the perfect excuse to reach down and pick him up. "Hey there boy, where are Midnight and Cleo?" she asked about his brother and sister, as if she expected him to answer her. She rubbed her cheek against his soft fur as she continued to pet him. "Brownies sure do smell good, Mom."

"Well, I got the buckeyes made over the weekend and did the rice krispy treats and some of the cookies yesterday. Today I finished the cookies and made the brownies. I think we will be ready for tomorrow evening. I thought I would have you help me with the cheese balls and the spreads tomorrow."

"Sounds good," Marie mumbled as she ate a Snickerdoodle from the plastic Tupperware container sitting on the counter. Her dad had gone back to the car and brought her bag in from the trunk. It was Dec. 23 and she would be staying until mid-morning on the 26th, when she and Tom would be leaving to go to Richmond and she would meet his parents.

Today?

Marie was stunned.

She and Tom had arrived in Richmond and had gone directly to The Executive Inn and registered as a married couple. It was early afternoon when they arrived. After hanging their clothes, they had gone down to the restaurant for a quick lunch. It was then that Tom had pulled out a small black box, taken out the ring, and had asked her to marry him. Today.

"Today? Are you seriously out of your mind?" She thought he was joking. "You know I will marry you," she said as she took the ring from his outstretched hand. She loved the ring. It was a large aquamarine, which was her birthstone, in the middle with two small pear-shaped diamonds on the side.

"Yes, today. All we need to do is go to the clerk's office and get a license, and the judge will marry us. I want us to be married before I leave."

"Is there something you aren't telling me?" she said as her brow furrowed.

"No. The war is coming to an end. I should be safer than I was as far as concerns there go. I just want to marry you. I want to know that we are connected in every sense of the word. I took you to bed because I love you, and I want you to know that love it true and deep."

"I already know that, Tom," she said gently as she laid her hand on his across the table.

The two heard conversations at the table next to them when they held hands. "And that is another reason. I want to make it public."

"Tom. You saw how my parents reacted to our laughing together. They let me know that they didn't understand how I could be so friendly with you since we were 'different.' I don't think they even realize how they sound. You and I are in the minority."

"Baby, I have always been in the minority. I am used to it," he said with a chuckle. "Now, finish up your soup and we are going to head out."

He looked at the ring on her hand and was pleased that she liked it so well.

"Where did you get the ring? I have never seen anything quite a lovely."

"I had it made in Saigon."

"You have had it all this time?"

"Marie, I had it made a year ago. I knew then I wanted to marry you. It was only a matter of time."

"Oh, Tom. Come on, we can eat soup later. It isn't every day a girl gets married."

The couple went to the room, showered, and were dressing when there was a knock on the door. Tom opened it and invited the woman in. "Marie, there is someone here for you," Tom said as he knocked on the bathroom door.

"What?" Marie asked as she entered the room in her robe, working on her hair.

She was greeted by a woman pulling a cart of beautiful dresses. "Captain Martin called and said you would be needing something appropriate for a late afternoon wedding and asked me to bring by some choices."

Marie's jaw dropped. Tom reached over, kissed her on the cheek, and told the woman to come see him in the lobby when they were finished. "My wedding gift to you, my beautiful bride. You have one hour, then we have an appointment downtown."

When Tom left, the women had a wonderful time. Marie picked the perfect dress on the first try, and they used the rest of the time to work on her hair and make-up. Elise, the young dress designer, remarked to Marie as they were finishing up, "Your guy seems so nice. It seems natural with you two, not like I thought it would be." She paused, "I'm sorry, I didn't mean it like that. I always thought it would be weird to be around a mixed couple, like..... I am messing this up. I have not ever been around black people. I thought they would be different from me, but they aren't, are they?"

Marie smiled, "No, they aren't. I never did even see Tom's color, if that makes sense. I did, but it was a difference that made no more difference than it did that he had brown eyes and mine are blue."

"Yeah, I get that now. I just saw a man who loved the woman he was going to marry and wanted her to have a happy day," she sighed. "That is all we want. Someone to love us."

Marie looked at the clock on the nightstand. "Well, this Cinderella needs to get busy. The clock is ticking, and I have about ten minutes before I turn into a pumpkin."

The young women both laughed and quickly put the finishing touches on Marie's hair. Elise took the clothes back out to the van before escorting Marie to the lobby.

Tom felt like all of the air had been sucked out of his lungs when he saw Marie come in the door. There had never been a more beautiful woman. He paid Elise, and the couple accepted her best wishes. She and Marie had exchanged addresses and vowed to keep in touch.

"You are the most beautiful bride I have ever seen," Tom said as he brushed a kiss on her temple and took her by the elbow to get into the car he had rented.

"Well, Captain," she said, emphasizing the "Captain," "You don't look too bad yourself. Now, let's get this show on the road. I want to celebrate this evening.... Just you and me.... Before we meet your parents tomorrow morning."

"Your wish is my command, my lady."

Tom had thought of everything. He had called ahead to have flowers delivered to the office so Marie had a corsage to wear. He looked very charming in his dress uniform and had arranged for a photographer to take some pictures to mark the occasion. Some day they would renew their vows in front of friends and family, but this day was the one that counted, and he wanted to make it special.

Wedding Night

Tom dug around in his duffel and found the three vanilla scented candles he had packed. He placed them on the credenza in front of the mirror and lit them.

He quickly stripped down and went to join Marie in the shower. The steam was filling the room as he opened the shower stall door. He stepped in and reached for her. "Mmmmm…" he said as he nuzzled her neck. "You smell so good." He then began kissing and nipping her shoulder. "You taste so good." He then reached around in front of her and as his hands found her slick folds he added, "And you feel so good."

She turned in his arms and put her arms up around his neck. "You are the only one who will ever smell me, taste me, or touch me. You have my promise." She pulled him down and met his lips with hers, and they opened for him to slowly enter her mouth with his tongue.

As the warm water poured down over them, they held each other closer. His hands went from her waist down around her apple-shaped cheeks as he cupped her ass and pulled her closer to him. She moaned as she felt his hardness slide in between her wet folds and she began rocking the length of him. She felt his tip tease her and she wanted to reach down and guide him inside her, but she enjoyed the building sensation far too much.

Tom pulled her closer and rocked along with her in a rhythm that he was certain would cause her to climax if he kept it up. Tonight he wanted her first climax to be with him deeply inside of her as they consummated their wedding vows.

He reached for the bar of soap and began running his hands all over her body to lather her up so they could get closer to getting to bed where he could slowly build her up to that final explosion. He got harder thinking about how he would taste her before she came with her muscles milking every bit of his juices out of him. His dick twitched once again as he thought of how she felt with that warm pussy for him to sink into.

"Oh, Marie," He pulled her to him again. "Let's rinse off and go to bed."

"That sounds perfect," she agreed as she got under the stream of steamy water to rinse off. She got out of the shower and began drying off. Tom realized if he was going to make this night last, he was going to release some of his tension or he would never last as long as he wanted to.

He began stroking himself and felt Marie step back into the shower and take over stroking as he pulled her close. "I wanted to be able to last for you, sweetie. I just about lose it when I even think about sinking inside you. I ---." He gasped as she wrapped around him tighter and began stroking him faster.

"Let me do this for you. Let me help you release that tension. Just play with my pussy while I do this."

She guided his hand to that warm wet spot between her legs and first his index finger entered her as she moaned, pushing her pelvis toward him as she continued her long strokes. She slowed the strokes as the second finger entered her and pushed in deeply, curving to find her sweet spot.

Marie felt like she was ready to explode as Tom pushed deeper and deeper. When he pushed deeply, found her spot, then stayed right there rubbing it until she could stand it no more, she stroked him faster and faster, telling him she was ready to come when he was.

"Now!" Tom exclaimed as he felt her muscles' uncontrollable contractions around his fingers as she convulsed. He came all over her hands as she caught the cum he shot out and rubbed his slickness back over his stiff cock.

Marie removed her hands and looked at Tom as she licked the remaining juices off her hand and he removed his fingers from inside her and did the same.

"You do realize we need to take another quick shower, don't you?" he laughed.

"If we don't watch it, we may never make it out of the shower," she responded.

The couple climbed into bed and relaxed into a restful sleep.

It was still dark when Marie rolled onto her back, only to be stopped by a warm body. Yes, she looked at her left hand, she was now Marie Martin. She nestled back against Tom's body, and he moved his hand around her waist and pulled her back closer to him.

"Good morning, Mrs. Martin," he mumbled as he nuzzled her neck and began nipping at her earlobe. His hands moved back to her lips and down her leg. He reached down and brought her leg back and over his thigh as his hand then went back to her lower lips and he began exploring her already moist folds. He found her little pearly nub and began circling it with his forefinger.

"Mmm," Marie said as she just relaxed at the feeling building in her. Her hips began rocking into his erection as his hands performed a rhythmic exploration. The rush was building inside her until it could no longer be contained and she gushed as she came.

"Damn! Woman. You are one hot mamma!" he said as he pulled her into a crushing hug.

Marie laughed as she rolled to meet him chest to chest and rubbed her wetness onto his cock and her hard nipples against him. She began an exploration of his chest with her lips and tongue as she went slowly down his body.

Tom gave a gasp when she licked the tip of his cock and slowly engulfed it with her lips then took him into her mouth. Her hands held his balls, and she massaged them while using the other hand to grip him at the base of his penis and sucked him with her mouth, moving up and down the length of him. His cock got harder and he felt the build up in his balls as he sensed his eminent release coming. "Marie, I am close," he told her, giving her the option of moving her mouth before he came. She moaned and continued the rhythm but just a bit faster and a bit deeper. He began pushing up into her mouth as he felt the release. "Oh, God, Marie," he shuddered as his seed went deeply in her mouth and she licked him clean.

They both laid back in the bed looking at the ceiling just thinking about the moment that had passed between them. His hand was on top of hers as they reached out to each other. "A lifetime of this. Now if that doesn't tell me I am in heaven, I don't know what would," Tom said quietly. "You are my heaven, Marie."

After removing her hand she rolled toward him and propped herself on her elbow as the other hand reached toward his chest. "We were meant to be, Tom. You know it. I know it. Now, we have to realize that not everyone else will see it. Your love makes me strong."

"Come here, Sweetie." He pulled her into a comfortable hug as they drifted off to sleep again.

Meeting the Martins

"Mom, Dad," Tom began, "This is Marie."

Marian Martin gave a look to first Tom, then Marie. "Thomas, she is every bit as beautiful as you told us she was. Come here, darlin," she said as she opened her arms to Marie.

Marie stepped into her hug and gave her a hug back. "You have raised a wonderful son."

"And she is smart too," Marian laughed. "Thank you. We tried to do our best. He hasn't caused us much grief, thank the good Lord above."

"Hey, there. I need to get my welcome in too," Tom's dad, James, interjected.

He held his hand out to take Marie's. He brought it up and kissed her knuckles. "Welcome to our home. We hope you enjoy your visit and consider our home your home any time."

Marie looked over and saw Tom's grin. "Well, at least now I know where you get your charm, Tom," she said with a laugh.

"Come on in and make yourself at home. Tommie tells us that you live in Ohio now but you are from Kentucky. What is your favorite good old southern meal?"

"Well, I am not really sure. My mammaw picks greens in the summer and I know that is southern. We have beans and cornbread with a piece of ham during the cold winter months, but other than that, I am not sure."

The Martins all laughed. "That is a good start, honey," Marian said.

They sat down to some of Marian's wonderful cooking. The meal included Southern fried chicken, fried cabbage, green beans, creamed corn and baked beans. The biscuits with chicken gravy on the side were wonderful, and Marie put butter and apple butter on hers. She was going to have to get some recipes so she could practice for the day when she had her own kitchen and could cook for Tom.

"Oh, wow," she said, sitting back and patting her stomach. "I think I am glad I have an elastic waistband or I would be unbuttoning my button like Tom is," she laughed as she watched him ease his hands out from under his sweater.

"Oh, dang, you caught me," he laughed as he thumped his stomach. "No one cooks like you do, Mamma. That was great."

"Y'all let that settle, and we have sweet potato pie for later when everyone is hungry again."

"You know. It is funny, isn't it. We are all so full now, but in about two hours we will be looking for something to snack on," James added.

Marie wouldn't take no for an answer as she helped Marian clear the dishes and get them washed, dried, and put up. She had a chance to observe the Martins and noted that there was an easy loving interaction as they engaged each other with humor.

"So, Son," James began, "how long do you get to stay?"

"I have to report back to Quantico on January third and I imagine it will be pretty soon after that. They want me to get back as soon as I can because they won't extend the deployment. Any day I am in the States is one day they have lost my war effort, if you get what I am sayin."

"Yep, they don't want to pay you if you aren't in the thick of things. Just like any other ole business."

"Yep, 'bout what it amounts to, Pop."

Marie noticed that even the accent and speech patterns of the trio changed as they spoke to each other and she was not included in the conversation. She found herself wondering if that would change, and she didn't think it would.

There was a cultural difference here that had nothing to do with the color of one's skin. It had to do with experiences. Her grandmother had a brother who had moved to California when he was young and had spent the rest of his life there. His children and his grandchildren had been raised there. When Marie and her parents had visited them years ago, it was like going to a different world. Her cousins not only spoke differently, but also they liked different kinds of music and enjoyed different activities. Yes, Marie had realized early in life that although people enjoyed life differently, they were all coming from the same place inside. She smiled as she went over to the table and sat down. "Do you play cards?"

"Do we play cards!" James laughed. "You bet your life little lady. We play Canasta."

Tom groaned. Marie could have suggested nothing better for his parents. They loved card games and were killers at Canasta. This would be a great way for all of them to do some bonding.

"And that gives us the win," said Marie, thirty minutes later, as she smiled across the table at Tom.

Tom got up and slapped his dad on the shoulder. "And that is why you never play cards with girls from Kentucky, Pop. They always win," He shot a grin and a wink at Marie.

Marian noticed the wink and, added to all of the other subtle looks and touches, she knew her son was deeply in love. It was something she had looked forward to since he had been a grown man. She liked Marie, but she had some reservations about a continuing romance between the two. There were some mixed couples in the family, so that was not really an issue. She just knew how much trouble those relationships had endured and she would withhold her reservations and wait to see how things progressed.

After a supper of leftovers, Tom and Marie left to go back to the motel. "Do you think they liked me okay?" Marie asked.

Tom reached over to take her hand. "I think they loved you. I just wish we could have told them we were together. They think I am going to take you to bed and make love to you, but they don't know that it means more than that."

"Yeah, I don't want them to think I just would go to bed with anybody."

"You and I know you were a virgin when we first got together. We are married now. It is none of anyone else's business. Not now, not ever."

"Yes," she said with a sigh, "I suppose you are right. No, I know you are right. It is just that everyone judges."

"The secret is just not to give a whip what they think."
She smiled, "That, Captain, is sometimes easier said than done."

Saying Goodbye

Tom and Marie had said their private goodbyes in their motel room all day on New Year's Day. While Marie had openly wept at the idea of being away from Tom for a year, he did not totally escape the sadness. His chest was heavy and his eyes held unshed tears that he would not be here with her, showing her how much he cared for her. For the first time he questioned his chosen career path.

The second came much too quickly as Tom drove her to the airport. She had planned on leaving at the latest possible time that would get her back home so she could be ready to go back into the classroom the next day.

They had arrived at the gate early so they would have some time together. The couple sat holding hands as Tom wrapped his arm around her shoulder and she rested her head on his chest. People did not sit in the chairs next to them but chose to stand instead. Marie noticed this and stood, pulling Tom up with her, and they went over to a more private area. "That is always what happens to you, isn't it?"

"Sometimes yes, sometimes no, but yeah, usually."

"I am so sorry, Tom. It shouldn't be that way."

"No, but it is what it is. It will be different one day, but not today. Now, you listen to me. I want you to go visit my parents this summer sometime. I already told them you enjoyed your visit and wanted to come back. I am going to talk to them before I leave. I will tell them I asked you to marry me and you accepted. They will know, but they will not have to deal with any of the issues until it is a reality in their world. You can do whatever you want to with your parents. Maybe they will come around and it won't be too bad."

"Yes, and maybe I will get a $2000 raise for teaching. Possible, but highly doubtful. I will be okay. I will mention you, and I will share your news with them when I get a letter." She then looked up at him from under her lashes, "At least I will share the parts that are not private." She then looked around to make sure no one was listening, "Will you write to me like you talk to me in bed? You know, dirty talk?"

Tom gave a loud laugh that caused a couple of people to glance their way. "Honey, you can read the letter in bed, and I will tell you so clearly what I want to do to you that you will be able to come from reading it." He pulled her in for another hug, kissing her hair and rubbing her back.

"Final boarding call for Flight 437. Final boarding call for Flight 437."

"Oh, Tom," Marie sobbed. "Stay safe. Tell Charlie hello and that I sent him a hug. I love you." She held on tightly until she had to break loose and get on the plane.

"I will write you as often as I can, Sweetheart."

"Me too." She walked over and handed her boarding pass to the attendant. She looked back one last time and watched him blow a kiss. She caught it, held it, and turned to walk back into her life.

My Darling Marie,

Charlie sends his love. Now, down to business. I arrived back here yesterday and found that two of the young boys who had attached themselves to our company in Xuan Loc had found their way here. Dinh Nghiem and Binh Chiem are now officially attached because they are seeking asylum in the United States. They have made their case at the Embassy and will be sent to the US sometime this month. They are both good kids and I hope they find a sponsoring family. If your church would want to sponsor one or both of them, we would certainly be gaining good citizens. I have written my parents with the same information. It is something that churches will be involved in as the war winds down. There will be so many refugees that will need to be relocated. It is sad.

How has your class been doing? Did you get signed up for the night class you were going to take? I know that one night a week the drive will not be too bad to Lexington unless the weather is bad. Please do not take a chance with your safety.

How are your parents? Have you had a chance to talk to them and let them know that you and I are writing to each other? I look forward to the time when I can go in your home, hand in hand, and sit with them like the family we are. Think about how wonderful it will be when we have babies for them to play with. My mother has talked about babies since I got out of the Academy. I think she wanted me to get the education and after that, she didn't care how soon I extended the family.

A friend of mine had his girlfriend move in with him, and my mom actually said that she thought that was a good idea for "young folks" to live together before getting married to see if they even liked each other. I never figured my mom to be a modern woman, but it appears I was wrong on that count. I remember when you just didn't live together without being married. Maybe I am growing up, but as much as I love you and want to live with you, I wouldn't feel right about that unless we were married. I am so lucky. I don't have to worry about that. I am putting the conversation for you in bed tonight on a separate page. You can get this out any time you want to feel me next to you or inside you.

My time is almost up so I will close for now. I love you more than I will ever be able to tell you or show you. You are my life, Marie Martin. (shhhh......) Love you, Baby.

Tom

My dearest Honey Bunny -

I couldn't resist, my darling husband. I heard someone use that phrase not too long ago. I laughed and laughed, and since it made me feel so good, I decided to share it with you.

The term is going very slowly, but it always does between Christmas break and Easter break. We usually have days in the fall that keep us getting breaks every once in awhile, but when January rolls around, we have short days combined with cold weather, and it keeps us inside and the time just seems to drag on and on.

What is your weather like? Of all the things we have discussed, I don't think that was one of them. You are in a tropical climate, so I guess you don't see much bad weather. I know there is a dry season and a rainy season. We don't think much about Vietnam other than how we are at war because of them. I guess that is unfair. We are not at war because of them. I am not sure why we are at war. I used to think it was to fight Communism. I am not sure any more.

134

On to a better topic. I fixed some fried cabbage like your mom fixed it. My parents really like it. I told them that I had gotten it out of a soul food cookbook. My mother asked, "What is Soul Food?" I may need to come visit you in Vietnam. What are some Vietnamese dishes? Shelly and Tabitha (she is back now, I guess you figured that) like it that I am practicing my cooking skills. They loved the sweet potato pie, and I found a recipe for a sweet potato souffle that we all enjoyed even more.

Your private letter was thorough and effective. I wish I could take it to school and laminate it so it wouldn't wear out. I just close my eyes and have it memorized. If you ever have a chance to get it recorded on one of those new cassette tape recorders, I would get one so i could play it and hear your voice while I do what you suggest. Now, that would be even better, if possible.

I sent you another care package. It has a special letter from me that you can use whenever you want to. Those big red lip prints let you see just how big i can open my mouth when it comes to taking you inside. I love you, Tom, and it seems like much more

than two months since you've been gone. I
might have some news for you next time I
write.

Love you always,
Your Marie

Nervous Expectations

Marie bit her lip as she sat filling out the papers at Dr. Foley's office. She left some of the blanks empty. She was not looking forward to the upcoming discussion. She had picked a doctor that was near her apartment. She had always gone to her family doctor, but this was not the time to go to Dr. McElroy.

"Mrs. Martin," the nurse called as she came out into the waiting room. Marie got up and followed the nurse back into the small examining room.

"You will need to get undressed and put this gown on," she said after getting Marie's weight and blood pressure taken. She left the room to give Marie the privacy she needed.

Dr. Foley entered the room a few minutes later after knocking before he opened the door. "Well, good afternoon, young lady."

Marie relaxed. He was in his fifties so he might be just who she needed to talk to. "Good afternoon," she replied as he took the forms she had filled out and began looking over them.

"Hmm… we will need your insurance information," he said as he looked up at her.

"That is the problem. I recently married a Marine who is now in Vietnam. I am not sure how to access that information since Tom is overseas.

"Well," the doctor responded. "Don't worry about that now. It looks like you only have the single coverage on your school plan, so I am sure your husband's veteran benefits will cover the rest. Now scoot up here and let's see if there is a little Martin in there."

The doctor examined Marie and swabbed for a couple of additional tests then left the room while she put her clothes back on. When he came back in he looked over her papers again to make sure all blanks were filled in. "I see you are married to a Negro."

She stiffened a bit, "Yes, a man of African heritage. Is there a problem?"

"No, not at all but there will be a test we will need to do later on for sickle-cell anemia. It occurs in those with a sub-Saharan ancestry, and we always like to test for it. It is unlikely your child would have it but we will check. It is a treatable blood disorder. It is more severe if both parents have the gene that carries it, but since you don't share the same ancestry chain that would be nearly a

138

zero chance." He patted her knee. "Don't worry. Do you have any questions at this time?"

Marie was so stunned she could only shake her head. Imagine, a baby. She and Tom were having a baby. "*Oh, my God!*" she thought again, "*Tom and I are having a baby. His parents don't know we are married. My parents don't even know we are seeing each other. Oh, my God.*" She began trembling.

"Are you okay?" the nurse asked. She had come in to give Marie prescriptions for prenatal vitamins.

"I will be when I get used to the idea. My husband and I had not planned on this happening quite so soon."

"How long have you been married?"

"Since December 27th."

"Well, that puts you into the month of October just barely. You will do fine." She then gave Marie instructions about the vitamins and an appointment card for her next visit.

Marie tromped to the car through the slushy remains of the snow that had fallen a few days ago. She had kind of hinted to Tom that there would be a surprise but she had thought that having Shelly take a picture of her in a couple of his favorite outfits would be what she would be sending. Now, she didn't know what to do.

What to Do Now

"You're WHAT?" Shelly said.

"Pregnant. I am pregnant. Now help me figure out what I am going to do," she said as she sat on the couch with a box of tissues on her lap.

"Well, you are going to have a baby, that is what you are going to do," Shelly sassed back. "What does Tom have to say?"

"I haven't had a chance to tell him. He tries to call once a month, and this next weekend is his scheduled call. I wanted to tell him in person rather than write a letter."

"That is probably the best," Shelly agreed. "How are you going to break the news to your parents? The idea that their unmarried daughter is having a baby isn't going to be good news. When they hear that the baby's father is a black man is really going to set off the fireworks."

"They won't have to process as much as that. Tom and I got married in December when we went to Richmond for me to meet his parents."

"You got married and didn't tell me? Why not, Marie?" Shelly looked surprised and hurt when she looked at Marie.

Marie reached over and touched her arm. "I didn't want you to have to lie about anything I was doing in case you were ever asked, that's why."

Shelly smiled, "As long as that is the only reason. Tom is a catch. He is a good looking guy who is head over heals in love with you. I am happy for you, and I am relieved that you are already married. That means that your medical expenses are covered and the baby will not be illegitimate. Let's face it Marie, being born out of wedlock is as bad to some people as being a mixed baby."

Marie gave her friend a look of understanding. "Yeah, I have really mucked it up."

"No, no. I didn't mean that," she reached over and hugged Marie. "You know I love you to pieces. I didn't mean anything personally. I was just talking about society."

"Yes," Marie began tearing up again. "That is exactly the problem. All of the whispers."

"Why would there be? You have a wedding ring, don't you?"

"Yes."

"Well, girl. Just put it on and stand proud. You will only be defeated if you let people make you feel like your love is something to be ashamed of."

Marie went into her bedroom and got the intricately carved Asian box that Tom had given her for Christmas. She opened the magic box, she slid the hidden panel to one side, and continued the puzzle. The lid popped open and revealed both her engagement ring and her wedding ring. She slipped them on after kissing them and returned to the living room to show Shelly.

"They are beautiful. This style is amazing."

"Tom brought them back from Saigon. He had them made before he was injured."

"Wow. He has been planning this for a long time." Shelly hugged her tightly again. "Whatever I can do to help you, let me know, okay?"

Marie nodded. They were both admiring the ring when Tabitha came bounding in the door. "Hey there, gals, what's up?" She came to a quick halt when she saw they were admiring rings on Marie's finger. "And what is that???" she squealed.

"I got married over Christmas break."

"You didn't! Oh, Marie!" She hugged her friend then stood back and looked at her again. "You married Tom? What are you going to tell your parents?"

"Yes, I married Tom," she said with a laugh. "We are also going to have a baby in October. I just found out today. As far as my parents go, I have no idea how to tell them."

"And, you have to decide what you are going to do at school," added Shelly.

"What do you mean?" queried Marie.

"Yeah," Tabitha piped in.

"Well, they need to know that Marie is married first. She will need to go through a name change and all of the hoops you jump through for that. Then, there are all the questions. No one has heard you talking about a boyfriend. There are all sorts of things to consider, but I have an idea."

Marie and Tabitha looked at each other, groaned, then they all began laughing. Shelly was known for some of her wacky ideas. But, strangely enough, most of them worked.

Phase One

After spending the weekend looking at every aspect of the situation, the three friends came up with a plan. They realized it might not be a good plan, but they vowed to stick with Marie until Tom came back from overseas. They would be her support system.

The first phase was for Marie to begin discussing Tom with the teachers at school. Shelly would drop his name at times, and then she would field questions that teachers would ask her. That is the thing about workplace gossip: You never ask the person directly; you always quiz their best friend to get all the information. They had all agreed that since it was now the end of March and school was out at the end of May, Marie would not do anything to announce her marriage or pregnancy.

As they went to school on Monday, they began talking about Tom in a way that indicated Marie had known him for a while and had been dating him. Shelly fielded the questions. He was a friend of a friend who had introduced him, and they liked each other and were going to be dating more steadily.

Anything beyond that was not necessary. They did not include information that Marie had met him a couple of years earlier and all that went into the relationship. It was a start to getting the information flow going.

Marie had looked into opportunities for transfer within the Cincinnati School System and found there were going to be openings in case she decided to apply for a transfer. She could do any paperwork for a name change over the summer and could go into a different school as a pregnant married lady. They were off and running until Marie got a call from her mother that her dad had fallen and was in the hospital.

Hospital Encounter

The three girls drove to Lexington over the weekend to visit with Marie's mom and give her some help with household chores while she and Marie visited her dad. It was while they were there that Marie had a situation develop that were going to cause her to rethink her position.

"Dr. McElroy. So good to see you. It has been a while," Marie said as she reached up to shake the doctor's hand.

"It has been. Have you found a doctor in Cincinnati yet? I can make some recommendations if you need one."

"I have a doctor I am going to now if I need any medical issues taken care of, but thanks," she replied. This was not a discussion she wanted to have in front of her mother, so she tried to change the topic of discussion. "How is Robbie? Did he decide to follow in the family footsteps?" she inquired.

"Yes, he did. He is ready to do his specialization in Ob-Gyn and will be working with a Dr. Foley at Methodist Hospital."

Marie felt the color drain from her face as she fought to gain control of her words,

"Well, that is great. Where is he living in Cincinnati?"

"He is on the east side. He thought that would be closer for him to get back home on the weekends. He has a girlfriend here. I tried to tell him he would be too busy to come home all the time, but he thinks he can do it. They are pretty serious about each other or I would still be trying to get the two of you together," he laughed.

Marie laughed too. Dr. McElroy and her mother had worked for years at trying to play matchmaker with their two children, only two years apart, but it had never developed into more than a great friendship.

"Well, I am glad Robbie is doing so well. Tell him hello when you see him next."

"You can tell him yourself," came a voice from the doorway. "I came to see dad and heard Mr. Sinclair was here, so I thought I would come and see him. This is a pleasant surprise," he crossed the room and Marie stood up and hugged him.

"You are looking almost doctorly," she said.

"Doctorly?" he laughed.

"Yes, doctorly."

148

"You kids go ahead and visit, Marie. Your mom and I will visit with the Doc for a minute," her dad said.

Marie and Robbie McElroy left and walked down the hall. "So, you are having a baby? Evidently your parents don't know."

"How did you know?"

"I am doing my work with Dr. Foley. I was reading over his notes and files getting my prep work done for the internship. I also read your side notes. Your situation is confidential so if you need to talk, I have a good ear."

"Oh, Robbie, it is getting so complicated. My parents don't know *anything* about it. They met Tom over the holidays when he was visiting Charlie's parents. He was injured in Saigon and was sent home to recuperate. He spent part of the holidays with them. I met him a couple of years ago and we fell in love. He proposed and we got married on Dec. 27th. My parents have no idea I am even dating anyone. They were not rude to him, but I am sure they have no idea that I would ever consider dating 'a Negro' as my dad would say. We wanted to wait until he was back into the States before we got our families involved in our relationship. I know it is still not something that is approved by lots of people."

"You're right there, and I must say that I am a bit surprised too. It doesn't make me think any less of you Marie," he added quickly as she looked at him sharply. "My girlfriend and I are intimate but if she were to get pregnant, we would get married. It is slowly changing, but some of the society issues will be slower to change than others."

Marie gave a big sigh and looked around to see that they had gone a circle and were back at her Dad's door. "Come on in and visit Mom and Dad for a minute."

After a few minutes, Dr. McElroy and his son left the Sinclairs to themselves to visit. It was when Marie and her mom were ready to leave that Brian Sinclair commented, "You know, Marie, you need to find you a nice young man like Robbie McElroy. He is smart. Has a good job and a good future. That is the kind of man you need to find."

Marie saw this as her opening. "I know, Dad. I actually have met someone like that. He is on a wonderful career path and has received several promotions in the last five years. He is extremely intelligent and very kind and considerate of others."

"You need to bring this young man around so we can meet him, then," Brian said.

Marie took a deep breath. It was now or never. "You already have met him, Daddy. It is Tom, Charlie's friend."

"Oh, Honey," her mother said.

"You can't be serious!" her dad bellowed then began coughing. He pushed the button for the nurse. "You can just forget that, Missy. Linda, talk some sense into her." He continued coughing, and Marie and her mom stepped out of the room.

"Oh, Marie. You can't date a Negro. What will everyone say? No, we just won't allow it."

"Won't allow it? Mother, I am not a little kid asking for permission to walk down the street to buy candy."

"Now, don't you take that tone with me!" her mother huffed. "We didn't raise you and send you to school so you could throw it all away and fall for someone of a different race. Think about how everyone would treat you."

"Oh, you mean like you are treating me now?" Marie responded with tears in her eyes.

"We are not going to discuss this any more. That young man was nice enough, but he is in Vietnam now. I am sure that he has forgotten all about meeting you, and you can certainly forget about meeting him. The discussion is over. Now let's get back in there and you treat your father with some respect. Apologize and tell him that you were just remarking that you thought that boy was nice. Understand?"

"Yes, Ma'am." At that time, Marie realized that her relationship with her parents had taken a turn that might survive but would never again be the close loving relationship she thought they had.

The Phone Call

Marie and Shelly were just getting back to the apartment when they heard the phone ring. Marie rushed to answer it, hoping it was Tom. It was Tom's mother instead. "Marie, have you heard from Tom?"

Marie's heart jumped into her throat, "No, ma'am, I was hoping he would have called over the weekend, but he didn't. Is something wrong?"

"No, dear, I am sorry if I scared you. There was a problem with the connections when he spoke with us. He asked that if you hadn't called by Wednesday for us to call you. He was going to ask if you would want to come and visit us over your Easter break. We would love to have you visit."

"I hadn't made any plans. I will need to think about it."

"You just take your time. Let us know your plans. We can pick you up at the airport."

Marie hung up and turned to Shelly. "Tom's parents invited me to come visit over our Easter break."

"Are you going?"

"I'm not sure. I haven't spoken to my parents in over two weeks. I called them several times and the conversation was limited. I decided they could call me next and they haven't. I don't know how to react to them. I think they are waiting for me to say that there is nothing I like about Tom and I was just speaking generally. I can't do it Shelly. I love him and I am married to him and I am having his baby. If I deny that, then pop up later and say... oops, guess what? Now, how hypocritical is that!"

"I don't envy you, that is for sure," Shelly responded.

Tabitha came in with her travel bag. "I am home until Sunday. What are we going to do this weekend?"

Marie looked over at her with a smile, "You are going to help me decide what to wear when I go visit Tom's parents."

"Really?" said Tabitha. "What happened?"

Marie explained that Tom's parents had called to invite her to visit upon Tom's suggestion and she was going to go. They were her in-laws--even though they didn't know it--and she wanted to get to know them better.

The Wednesday before Easter, school was out and vacation had begun. Marie had four days, and Shelly took her to the airport.

"If my parents call, tell them I am visiting friends and that I will be back Sunday evening after 7:00 if they want to call back. You have my number out there if there is an emergency."

The girls hugged, and Marie got onto the plane with butterflies in her stomach. She hoped it was a good visit. She had written to Tom that she would be going to his folks and that she hoped he would wait until she got back home before he called. She let him know that she had something important to talk to him about but she did not hint about what it was.

Getting to Know the In-Laws

"Marie, over here," James shouted as he waved his hands over his head.

Marie smiled and waved back as she made her way over to James and Marian Martin. Marian engulfed her in a hug the stood her back and took a look at her. "You look beautiful. We will talk later," she said mysteriously.

They made their way through Richmond to the house where James unloaded Marie's suitcase from the trunk and carried it in.

Conversation flowed easily between the threesome. Marie helped Marian with supper, and the conversation let to discussing Tom. "So, have you told Tom he is going to be a daddy yet?" Marian inquired.

Marie's face reddened. "How did you know?"

"Honey, I know how the two of you looked at each other over you Christmas holiday that you were in love. I confess I worry about how your love will be accepted by other people, but I am just glad Tom found a wonderful woman to love. Now, have you told him?"

"No. I was going to tell him last month but we didn't get our call. I did tell him in a letter that I had something to tell him. I am just about three months pregnant now. I wish he were here, so I could tell him in person."

Marin reached over and patted her hand. "It will all be okay, and he will be thrilled. Tom always has always wanted a family and children. You need to find a way for the military to get you two married as soon as you can."

Marie didn't want to tell Tom's parents they were already married but it seemed that she had no choice. "We took care of that when we were here. We were married on December 27th."

Marian jumped up from the chair where she sat drinking a cup of coffee, "Oh, Marie. I am so happy. You are the daughter we never had. James," she called into the living room, "Come in here. James?"

"Yeah, I'm coming, I'm coming," he said as he entered the kitchen. "What's going on?"

"Tom and Marie got married when they were here in December and we are going to have us a grandbaby, that is what."

James went over and hugged Marie, "Bless my soul. Do you kids know what you are getting yourselves into?"

"James," said Marian as she swatted his arm. "Don't be like that! Be happy for them."

"Well, of course, I am happy," he turned to Marie, "I couldn't be happier, I just know you aren't going to have an easy time of it."

Marie responded, "I am sure we are going to have the same adjustments as any newly wedded couple who finds themselves headed for parenthood so quickly."

"What do your mother and father have to say about it?" Marian asked.

"My parents don't know. I tried to tell them about Tom a month ago, and it didn't go well."

Marian patted Marie's arm again. "You just try not to worry, it will all work out. It always does. The good Lord doesn't give us more than we can handle, and if you lean on him, it will all be okay."

The rest of the visit was enjoyable as they discussed boys' names and girls' names. James and Marian assured Marie that they would help them in any way they could. When Tom got back stateside he had no idea where he would be stationed and there would be lots to work out.

"My biggest regret is that he will not be here to share the baby."

"Well, you will just have to take a lot of pictures. He will want to see you as you grow round with his baby. Trust me on that one," said James as he came into the kitchen.

My wonderful wife,

Marie, I needed to write to let you know how excited I am by the news you shared. I was so surprised when you told me that I am not sure I reacted well. I am thrilled that we are having a baby. I had not expected it so soon, but that is of no concern. I just am trying to figure out how I can be part of the experience.

I have so many questions about it. Have you told anyone we are married? I want you to let people know that. I do not want them to make any judgements on you for getting pregnant without being married. You can just tell people that we were married in December. That is all they need to know.

What have your parents said? My parents are excited too.

I have been thinking about your teaching job. I make enough with my pay that you can give up your position at the end of the year if you want to. It is entirely up to you on that. I will not be home until the end of the year, and I only hope I get there before Christmas. I will not be there for the birth of the baby and that saddens me. I hate that you are alone during all of this. I want to share the feeling of our baby kicking and how beautiful you look as you get bigger and bigger with him or her growing inside of you. I love you so much, Marie. I don't even know how to tell you. You are my day and my night. You are my sunshine and my life. I never would have thought I could love someone this much, but I do.

I have an idea if you want to think about it. If the baby is due in October, you might want to just take a year of teaching off. It would give you time before the baby to just relax and prepare for motherhood. After he or she is born, it would give you time, almost a year, before you would have to begin the school year again. By that time, I will be home and we will know where we will be living and you could apply for a teaching job wherever we live. Think about it.

I love you but I need to get going. I will call you as soon as I can.

All my heart is yours,   Tom

My own true love, forever,

It was so good getting your letter. Your reaction to the news was about like mine, shock. Your parents have been great. I get a call from you mother every week. I have only heard from my parents once in the last month. School will be out soon but I want them to know before that. I have plans on going to Lexington this next weekend.

You know I mentioned you as being a possibility of a good man to be in love with. They have had time to digest that because I refused to take it back as my mother suggested. I hope they accept you, but if they don't Tom, that is their choice. I will deal with that when the time comes. If they don't accept it now, then I can only hope they accept it when the baby gets here.

I am thinking about your suggestions on taking a year off. It sounds reasonable to me. I am not showing yet, but my clothes are a bit snug and yesterday I couldn't get my jeans buttoned. That is to be expected, I guess, but it seemed strange. We have about a month of school left and I think I can get through that without having to change my wardrobe.

As far as letting people know I am married, Shelly is going to take care of that and just explain that I didn't want to go throught the name change and confuse the kids at school. I want my parents to hear it first. I know it is kind of lame, but we think it will work okay. We will wait until the last day of school to announce it. If you are sure that we can meet the bills I have with your salary, I can do that. I could also substitute teach during that time for some additional income.

Call me when you can. I love you Tom. I can hardly wait to feel your arms around me and watch you hold our son or daughter.

All my love always,
Marie

Telling the Folks

"Marie, you are going to have to settle down. You are as nervous as I have ever seen you."

"I know," said Marie as she was literally shaking as she anticipated her conversation with her parents.

"I will stay in the living room as you take your folks into the kitchen. I don't think they will yell and carry on with me in the other room, but if they do, I will come in and tell them we are going and that I will come back with you when they have calmed down. You don't have to tell them about the baby this trip. Just let them know that you got married in December."

"I know," Marie repeated as she calmed down.

Shelly pulled into the Sinclair driveway. Wes and Brian were shooting hoops as Sandra and Linda were planting matching planters to be placed at their back doors. The families had always been close and now Marie was hoping on Charlie's parents to be supportive since Tom was one of Charlie's best friends.

"Hi, Wes, Sandra," she called as she got out of the car. "This is my friend and roommate, Shelly."

"Hello, Shelly, it is nice to meet you," Sandra said.

"Nice meeting you all too," Shelly replied.

"Mom, Dad. You are both looking good," Marie said to her parents.

"Hi, Honey," said her mom, "I am glad you had time to come visit. Hello Shelly. I just baked some brownies this morning. You girls want some?

"Sure," Marie replied. It would get them in the house and in the kitchen.

They went in the back door and Shelly excused herself to use the bathroom. She would then stay in the living room to give Marie a chance to share her news with her mother.

"Ah, Mom," Marie began. "Let's just sit down a minute and talk. We can have brownies in a little bit."

"Is something wrong, Honey?" Linda said with concern.

"No, not really. I just had some news I wanted to share with you and Daddy."

"Well, let me call him in here," She went to the kitchen window. "Brian, can you come here a minute?"

Linda went ahead and cut the pan of brownies while they waited for Brian to come in the house.

"Okay, what's going on?" Brian asked as he looked from Linda to Marie.

"I wanted to tell you," she began. "I wanted to let you know," she started again.

Linda sat down and put her hand on Marie's. "You want to tell us what?" she said as she looked up at Brian.

"I got married to Tom in December!" she blurted out.

"Goddammit! Tell me you didn't marry that nigger!"

"Brian," admonished Linda. "Don't use that word! She can just get it annulled and no one will ever know. He is in Vietnam and he can't be here to contest it. We will call Bill Fortner. He has been our lawyer for years, he will know how to handle this."

Brian went to the counter, opened one of the drawers, and pulled out the phone book. He opened it then reached for the phone as Marie said, "No, I will not get it annulled. As a matter of fact, it would not be possible since I am pregnant."

Linda and Brian looked at each other then back at Marie.

"Get out," said Brian as Linda began crying. "Go back to Cincinnati, where there are lots of Negroes who will take you and your black baby in. Don't bring that nigger or your nigger baby here. We thought we had raised you better than this."

Marie was sobbing as Shelly came in the kitchen. She gave Marie's parents a glare as she went over and put her hands on Marie's shoulder in support. "Let's go, Marie. You wanted to visit with Charlie's parents before we went home. Let's go."

"No," said Brian. "You will not go over there. You will leave now."

"Daddy, I love you and Mother, but I will go visit Wes and Sandra. Charlie has been my friend my whole life and he is a good friend of Tom's. You can kick me out of the house I grew up in, but you cannot keep me from visiting Charlie's parents. I will get out of here and out of your life. You just remember that you are going to have a grandchild and you are choosing to toss me and that child

166

out. If you ever change your mind, I will welcome you back into my life, but I will not beg you to love me or the baby."

They went to the door and Marie looked back one last time before they crossed the drive to the Johnson's.

Charlie's Parents

"Honey, honey," Sandra Johnson said as she held Marie in her embrace, "Your mom and dad will come around. They are surprised. Shoot, kiddo, I am surprised too. Does Charlie know?"

"I imagine he does now. Since we are having a baby, I imagine Tom told him. Oh, Sandra. What am I going to do? I knew my parents would not be pleased, but I never thought they would kick me out of their life."

Wes entered the room as they were speaking. "Lynn Marie, your folks are good people. Until we met Tom we had ideas about how black folks were. We were wrong. You visit us any time. Your mom and dad will see that baby and their hearts will melt. It may take them some time, but they will come around."

"I hope you are right. This is breaking my heart." Marie continued to sob. "Shelly and I need to get home. I have some decisions to make now that I know how they feel."

"I fixed lasagna for supper. You girls stay and eat. We haven't seen you for a while, and we have missed you. As a matter of fact, we just got a letter from Charlie yesterday. He talks like the fighting has slowed down a lot. Does Tom talk much about the war? Charlie doesn't say much to us, he just tries to tell us it isn't as bad as what we are seeing on television. I think he does that so we won't worry about him."

"Tom doesn't say much about the war either. We have just been so busy talking about our lives and what things we need to do to be ready for his return. Now, we have the baby to talk about."

"Oh, let me get a picture of you and Shelly to send Charlie then he can share it with Tom. I will get two copies made. I will even take one of you by yourself for Tom to carry with him."

"He had a photographer take one of our wedding that I have on my night stand. I love him so much, Sandra. Does that make me a bad person?"

"No! Don't you ever think that. We don't choose who we fall in love with. Ten years ago, people would go nutty if a Protestant married a Catholic. When President Kennedy was elected everyone thought that would mean that the Pope would be running the United States. There are always going to be crazy people with crazy ideas, but sometimes all it takes is just a little bit of knowledge to make folks change their minds. I am not sure your mom and dad will ever mention anything to us, but if they do, you know we love Tom like a son and we will tell them so. Your job for the next few months is to just relax and take care of yourself and that baby."

School's Out

Shelly, Tabitha, and Marie sat to rest outside Lazarus in the new mall. The women loved the shopping there, but Marie noticed that she tired more easily since school had ended.

"You are getting some cute tops," said Tabitha.

"Thanks," said Marie. "I just wish we could find a store that had some maternity clothes that looked more fashionable. I will just put these tops with black pants, I guess."

Marie and Tom had decided that she would wait until August and apply for a year's leave from teaching. She would be able to do some substitute teaching on days she wanted to, but she could just use the time to prepare for the baby.

Although Tabitha and Shelly had assured her that there would be room for the baby at the apartment, Marie had applied for her own apartment in the complex. She knew that a baby would require more space than their apartment had. Her friends assured her that they would be right there to help her until

Tom came home, regardless of where she lived.

While they were carrying packages in, the phone began ringing. Tabitha quickly picked up the receiver, "Hello?"

"Hello. Is Lynn Marie Sinclair home?" the voice queried.

"Um.... yes?" she answered as she looked over at Marie. "Did you want to speak with her?"

"Yes, please," the gentleman answered with a chuckle.

"Marie, this guy sounds HOT," Tabitha grinned as she handed Marie the phone receiver.

"Hello?" Marie said a bit hesitantly.

"Marie, this is Robbie."

Marie sighed. "Oh, Robbie, hi there. How are you, is anything wrong?"

"No, not at all. Who answered the phone? She sounds hot."

Marie laughed. "I will have to introduce you sometime. Why don't you come over this evening. I think we were planning on just ordering a pizza."

"That sounds great, I have the evening off. What time would be good? I have a couple of things that have come up that I wanted to tell you about."

"Just come on over after the office closes, and I will see you then."

They said their goodbyes, and Marie let Tabitha know that they would be having company. Tabitha ran off to get ready to meet the guy who owned that deep rich voice that set her girly parts fluttering.

House Call

It was a little after 7:00 when the doorbell rang. Marie opened it up to find a casually dressed Robbie McElroy leaning on the door jam.

"You look great!" he exclaimed as he stood and entered the apartment. "You are one of those women who glows when pregnant. How are you feeling? I saw that you aren't due in for a visit for another couple of weeks."

"I am doing great," Marie answered. "I get tired sooner. And I had to pick up some new pants today. Other than that, I am fine."

"If you are like most women, you will look pregnant as soon as you put on that first pair of maternity pants. Most women tell me it is the best thing they decide to do. Why don't you go slip into a pair now and put on a loose top and see how you feel."

"Hahahah," she laughed. "I have been thinking about doing that very thing since we got home. I'll be right back." She turned to go back into her bedroom as Tabitha entered from the hallway.

"Hey, Marie," she began then stopped as she noticed Robbie. "Oh, excuse me, I didn't realize our company was already here." She smiled at Robbie and extended her hand. "I am Marie's roommate, Tabitha. Tabitha Wells. Nice to meet you."

"You two get to know each other while I change clothes."

Robbie and Tabitha had just begun talking when Shelly bounded in the door with the pizza. "Hey, everybody," she called before realizing that Robbie and Tabitha were sitting on the couch. "Oops. Excuse me."

Tabitha got up to take the pizza. "Shelly, this is Marie's friend, Robbie. Robbie, our other roommate, Shelly."

Robbie rose to shake hands with Shelly. "Hello, Shelly, it's good seeing you again."

"You too." Shelly explained to Tabitha, "Robbie and I met at last week's doctor's appointment. He is interning with Dr. Foley."

The group shared interesting stories that ran from medical craziness to travel bits and the state of education. It was a lively conversation full of laughs. Before they realized it, it had grown dark. Robbie thanked them for the pizza and the entertainment then rose to leave.

"Why did you call me this afternoon, Robbie," Marie asked, realizing she had not thought any more about the reason for his call.

"Walk me to my car and we can chat about that," he replied.

Marie started the conversation as they walked to the car. "You were right about going ahead and getting into my new maternity clothes. I feel so much more comfortable, and when I looked in the full mirror, I am beginning to look pregnant. Thanks."

"You will notice the stomach will become more relaxed within a couple of days. You are over five months pregnant, so it is natural for that baby to take up more room," he advised, then added, "'Have you heard from your folks, Marie?"

"No," she sighed. "I had hoped I would by now, but nothing. Why do you ask? There isn't anything wrong with them is there?"

"Not that I am aware. I was in Dad's office the other day when your mom and dad came in. They were not their usual enthusiastic selves. Have you told them about the baby?"

"Yes, I am sure that is why they are not looking enthusiastic," Marie said while she unknowingly clinched her hands, a reaction that Robbie did not fail to notice. "They sent me out of the house about a month ago and told me to take my n... , I can't even say the word, baby with me." Marie took a deep breath. She was all cried out. She had no tears left for the parents she had always tried to obey and make proud of her.

"They will come around. They will, I am sure. You just try not to get upset."

"My days of worrying about what people think about me is at an end. Right now, all people will see is a pregnant lady. I am married, so at least that is not an issue. Once they see me with a little dark-skinned baby, it may not be that easy to ignore, but for now, it is."

"I will see you in a couple of weeks at the office, if not before. If you need me, for any reason, just give me a call. You know, Charlie and I ran around as friends together for years when we were all growing up. You and he are like family and I am looking

177

forward to meeting your husband and his good friend, Captain Martin. You hang in there."

He and Marie lightly hugged before he got into the car and drove off.

"Wow," said Tabitha as Marie came back into the apartment. "I wanna go out with that guy. Do you think I stand a chance?"

"I don't know why not. If he doesn't call you, call him with an idea of somewhere you want to go but don't have a date. You'll think of something."

"You can go with Marie for her next doctor's appointment if you are in town," Shelly chimed in.

The women cleared the living room of clutter then went about their nightly rituals of preparing for bed.

My darling Tom,

I am getting as big as a barn. I miss you so much, but I am glad you are not here to see me. The baby is amazing as it moves inside me. Sometimes I can see an elbow sticking out when it turns. I hate to keep calling it an "it."   I will just call the baby Barbara John.

I got a letter from Charlie. He said he had been sent out to some other cities over there for some kind of "field work." Whatever that means, I hope it is not dangerous. He said that troop movement had slowed down, but I am not sure quite what that means. I know there is little that either one of you can tell me about your lives over there. I just hate getting my information from the news stations. I think they want us to keep hating, and I am finding it harder and harder to do. I think there has been a lot of manipulation going on by our government in the situation.

Do you have an idea of when you will be mustered out and back home? Did you ask for an early release since the baby is coming? I only ask because I am curious about whether or not to sign a year's lease at the new apartment. I can get a one bedroom unit in the same building I was in with the girls. It is a first floor apartment so that will be great. Let me know how you feel about it. I can sign a lease and move in at the first of October if we decide to go with it. Since I have already lived here, I will not have to pay a security deposit nor will I have to pay the last month's rent. It will make it much more affordable. You can let me know when we next talk.

I talked to our pastor about sponsoring the Vietnamese woman and her son that you spoke of. She seemed to be someone that would be a worthy person to sponsor to come to the country. I will need for you to send me more information but the committee agreed that it was a worthy cause and they will give it full consideration.

Love always, Marie

Marie, my Marie,

I ache for you. I am counting down the days until our baby gets here. We have, what, a month left before Barbara John makes an appearance? I am only sorry I will not be there for the birth. I would never have thought that I would be so disappointed about something like that, but I am.

Did you get the lease signed okay? I want you to hire someone to help you get moved. I know it is only from upstairs down, but you and your friends do not need to be doing all of that heavy lifting. Enclosed is a check. I know you have had your salary over the summer, and I appreciate that I have been able to save since we married. This check is my extra pay for combat and the amount I would have been spending if I had been in a civilian job, paying for my rent. It is a tidy sum and should cover everything you need until I get home in December or January.

I have been working on some communications with Annapolis. There is a chance that I might be able to get a one year stint as strategist instructor. My two years of being in the field here and the commendations I received when I was in Xuan Loc will serve to help me get the position. Keep your fingers crossed, Baby. That would be great. Is your landlord willing to do a six month lease instead of a year? Maybe if you explained the situation to him and he collected that last month's rent up front he would even go for a month to month lease. Check your options.

I am sending you a gift. It is a keepsake box for the baby. It will actually have the name Barbara John in Vietnamese as part of the carved decoration on the lid of the box. I thought that would make for an interesting story for our son or daughter when they were grown, recounting what it meant when our grandchildren asked them. What do you think? Too corny? It is agarwood, which is not easily available and expensive but I helped a native and his family avoid capture, and he wanted to make it as a gift to our baby. That will make it even more special, I think.

Gotta go, Sweetheart, I love you so much,

Tom

Happy Birthday

"Grab the suitcase," Shelly shouted to Tabitha.

"Yes, I have it," she replied. "Let's get Marie down to the car and to the hospital."

"Hey, I am fine. I really am," Marie laughed. "I just know that Robbie said if contractions began at night and were less than five minutes apart for me to get to the hospital. The baby is about a week overdue so it probably won't be a false alarm at this stage."

Shelly had the car started and, as soon as the other two were in, they took off for the hospital. It seemed to them as though every light would turn red as the space between Marie's contractions got closer and closer.

By the time they pulled into the hospital's parking lot, they had decided that probably they needed to go through the emergency entrance and get Marie in the facility as soon as they could. Her contractions were about three minutes apart, and none of them wanted to take any chances of having her walk across the parking lot and end up with a problem.

Tabitha went in, explained the situation, and came back out with an attendant pushing a wheelchair. They helped Marie out of the car and Shelly went to park while the others went in and began the admittance process. Robbie had arranged her pre-admission so it was a relatively quick process before she was on her way to the maternity ward.

Marie was on her way to her room when her water broke. The nurses scrambled to get her into a gown and to the labor room. Tabitha and Shelly went to the waiting room while the nurses took care of Marie. She had opted for a natural birth and would have an epidural only if there was a problem. Robbie had gone with her to birthing classes, so Tabitha had called him before they had left the apartment. He met Marie in the labor room and advised that Dr. Foley was on his way to the hospital.

"Okay, breathe. Short breaths like we practiced, remember," said Robbie. "That's it. Just do that again."

Marie went from being a bit anxious to being in command of her breathing. She was concentrating on that rather than the pain she was feeling. She had been shaved and prepped and all that was left to do was breathe and wait.

"Nurse," Robbie said as the nurse came by the cubicle. "You need to let Dr. Foley know it will be pretty shortly. Contractions are coming about a minute apart and she measures eight centimeters."

"Yes, Doctor," the nurse replied and went to get the delivery room ready.

"Hold my hand and squeeze whenever you need to. Just listen to me coach you with your breaths, and we will get little Barbara John here as easily as we can."

"You have got to be kidding. This kiddo has already kept me waiting a couple of weeks. I think he is as ready to be born as I am to see him."

"Him?" the nurse queried.

"I have decided it is a boy," Marie laughed as another contraction began.

"Okay, begin pushing."

Less than ten minutes later, the nurse was laying Jonathon Allen Martin in Marie's arms. She pushed the soft receiving blanket to the side and saw the most adorable baby. A full head of curly dark hair and a scrunched up look on his face that said, "Get that light out of my face." His little fists opened and grabbed her finger as she reached toward him.

"Jon, you are just the perfect little guy," she crooned. His fist found his mouth and he began working his mouth.

"He is hungry. We need to take him to get him fed. You will be able to feed him later today. Right now, you need to rest." The nurse took the baby to the nursery and Marie was wheeled to the recovery room. Since she had been able to have a totally natural delivery, she was actually ready to get up and out of bed. The nurses, however, made certain she stayed in bed for an hour before getting her back to her room.

When she got into the room, Shelly and Tabitha were waiting with balloons and presents. Robbie came in with flowers. "Oh, Robbie, they are beautiful. Thank you."

"I wish I could take the credit, but they aren't from me."

"Let me see the card." Marie's hands shook as she opened it.

"To the greatest love of my life, Tom."

"Oh!" Marie's hand flew to her mouth. "How did he know?" She looked at Robbie and he grinned.

"I had been corresponding with Charlie and asked him if there was a way that a man could be contacted when his wife had a baby. We had this information tree set up that I started when the girls called me that you were in labor. The only call we had left to make was the one to Tom. He had already made arrangements for the specific flowers he wanted you to have. He knows he is a daddy, and he and Charlie both gave permission for me to hug you and give you a kiss on the temple only."

They all laughed then looked at the door as the nurse came in carrying the baby.

Marie opened her arms to hold the baby and the rest of the early morning hours were spent expounding on the perfection of the little baby they were all so pleased to see.

Marie was tiring. Robbie had to get to the office, Shelly needed to get to work and Tabitha had a flight out later in the day. They all took their leave.

When the nurse came in, Marie asked for just one more minute. She looked down at

Jon and said, "Your daddy loves you very much and will get home to us as soon as he can. The next time I see you, I want to tell you all about him." She then leaned down, kissed him, and handed him to the nurse.

She fell asleep thinking about her life, the turns it had taken, and relished the idea of adventures to come.

Epilogue

"Oh, Tom," Marie said as she looked at the beautiful ring that she had received for Christmas. "This is one of the most beautiful rings I have ever seen."

"Here, Baby," he said, taking it from her and placing it on the ring finger of her right hand. "This marks fifty years of love, you know? We have had some great times, that is for sure."

"And our share of trials, too," she said as she put her arms around his neck and reached up to give him a kiss.

"And….. I still treasure every one of those kisses you can give me."

"Wonder how many kisses we have managed over the last fifty years," Marie said, laughingly. "If we had a dollar for everyone, we would be wealthy indeed."

"I think they have been worth much more than a dollar each. Now, let's get dressed before the kids walk in on their folks in a private celebration."

The couple showered and changed into their clothes. Marie could still fit into the dress she wore fifty years ago, and Tom looked splendid in his uniform. He had more bars then he had fifty years ago, but the results were still the same: the two made a striking couple.

"Are you ready?"

"You betcha, Baby."

Tom offered Marie his arm and the two walked out of their hotel room and toward the elevator. A nearby door opened as a young girl ran out and lunged at Tom's leg. "Pappaw. Mommie won't let me take Marshmallow Head to the wedding."

Tom got down even with the beautiful little girl and gave her a hug. "Dumplin," he began, "Marshmallow Head wants to stay in the room and rest up for the big meal after the wedding. He told me that earlier today and I gave him permission to, if that is okay with you."

"Aw… I guess so, if you told him it would be okay." The little girl turned and went back through the door she had burst out of.

"I swear, Tom, you have all those grandbabies and great-grandbabies eating out of your hands."

Tom and Marie reached the elevator and pushed the button that would take them down to the medium-sized banquet room that had been rented for them to renew their vows on their fiftieth anniversary. It had been planned by their five children, and they were looking forward to seeing everyone gathered together for the first time in ten years.

They walked through the door and were greeted by Jon, their oldest, and the twins, Cindy and Sarah.

"Mom," Sarah said, "You look absolutely gorgeous."

"Thank you dear. Did I ever tell you about the history of this dress?"

"I think so, but wait until my girls are here so they can hear the story." Sarah turned to see who had just entered the room and saw their younger brother, Art, with his wife and three kids, all with spouses and grandchildren. It was turning into a great gathering and Tom and Marie looked at each other and smiled.

"Is everyone about here?" Tom asked John. "I am as anxious to marry your mother as I was fifty years ago."

"Calm down, Dad," Jon laughed. "We are waiting for Jenny and her crew and we will be all set."

The children, grandchildren, and special new great grandchild all had gathered for this special moment in their life.

Tom looked around then turned to Marie. "Do you see what I see?"

"Yes, I see a field of beautiful flowers, all different colors, all shades resulting from our collective passions in the last fifty years."

Tom put his arm around Marie's waist and pulled her toward him, giving her a passionate kiss. "Speaking of passion, let's get hitched. I am ready for the honeymoon," he said with a laugh as they walked down the aisle to pledge their love once again.